W9-ADG-161
WITHDRAWN
ANOTHER
DAY AS
Emily

ALSO BY EILEEN SPINELLI

The Dancing Pancake

Summerhouse Time

ANOTHER DAY AS Emily

EILEEN SPINELLI

ILLUSTRATED BY JOANNE LEW-VRIETHOFF

A YEARLING BOOK

 Published in the United States by Yearling, an imprint of Random House Children's Books, a division of Random House LLC, a Penguin Random House Company, New York. Originally published in hardcover in the United States by Alfred A. Knopf, an imprint of Random House Children's Books, New York, in 2014.

Visit us on the Web! randomhousekids.com

Educators and librarians, for a variety of teaching tools, visit us at
RHTeachersLibrarians.com

The Library of Congress has cataloged the hardcover edition of this work as follows:
Spinelli, Eileen.
Another day as Emily / Eileen Spinelli ; illustrated by Joanne Lew-Vriethoff. —
First edition.
p. cm.
Summary: "Susie is jealous when her brother is deemed a town hero, so she finds solace in the poetry and reclusive lifestyle of Emily Dickinson." —Provided by publisher
ISBN 978-0-449-80987-7 (trade) — ISBN 978-0-449-80988-4 (lib. bdg.) —
ISBN 978-0-449-80990-7 (ebook)
[1. Novels in verse. 2. Family life—Fiction. 3. Dickinson, Emily, 1830–1886—Fiction. 4. Recluses—Fiction. 5. Self-acceptance—Fiction.] I. Lew-Vriethoff, Joanne, illustrator.
II. Title.
PZ7.5.S68An 2014 [Fic]—dc23 2012043105

ISBN 978-0-449-80989-1 (pbk.)

Printed in the United States of America
10 9 8 7 6 5 4 3
First Yearling Edition 2015

To Barbara Rosencrans
and Linda Steen

ACKNOWLEDGMENTS

Writing is a solitary thing, and yet I've never written a book entirely by myself.

My grandson Will Merola researched nineteenth-century baseball for me. A peek behind the curtain into the world of theater was furnished by my friend and playwright Y York. My friend Patty Beaumont told me how one catches a chipmunk on the loose.

If you like this book, you should note the name Michelle Frey, my editor—and her assistant, Kelly Delaney—and add your thanks to mine.

And my sweet husband, Jerry, has once again done his duty as First Reader.

ANOTHER DAY AS Emily

EMERGENCY

Mrs. Harden nearly died today.
I know because I was there.
I saw her slumped
on her kitchen floor
looking white as an egg.
I wasn't there
from the beginning, though.
Only from the time
my little brother, Parker,
went missing.

THE BEGINNING

It seems Parker wanted to
drive somewhere
on his new trike.
He's only allowed to go
one house up
each way.
And only if he tells someone
where he's going.
He obeyed the first rule.

(Mrs. Harden lives next door.)
But he forgot the second rule.
He told no one.
He drove to Mrs. Harden's.
He parked in her driveway.
He knocked at her back door.
She invited him in
for a cookie.
That's how it started.

THE SPELL

Before Mrs. Harden
could reach the cookie jar,
she had what grown-ups call
"a spell."
Parker saw her collapse.
He remembered his safety lessons.
He climbed on a chair.
He reached for the phone.
He dialed 911.
This is where I come in.
I find him

shouting to the dispatcher:
"Emergency! Emergency!"

HELP IS ON THE WAY

I'm here because
Mrs. Harden and I
are supposed to paint posters
for her women's club bake sale.
Paints and rags and poster board
are sitting on her craft table.

Mrs. Harden and I do lots of
projects together.
She is sort of an honorary
grandmother to me.
(My real ones live across the country.)

I crouch on the floor
next to her.
I take her hand.
It's cold and clammy.
I pat it.

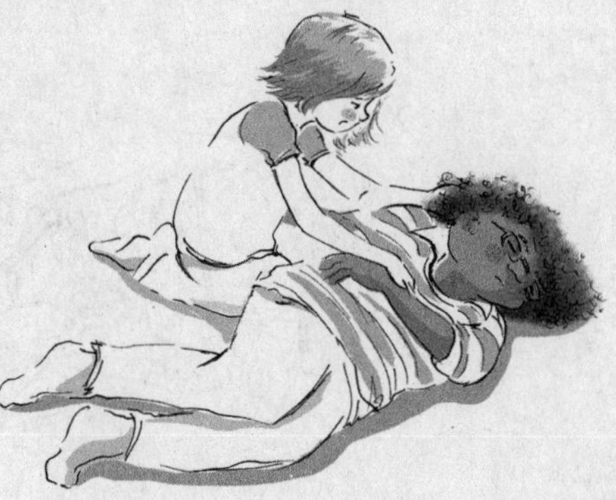

"It's me. Suzy," I tell her.
"Don't worry, Mrs. Harden. Help is on the way."

THE LITTLE HERO

The ambulance comes.
The EMTs wheel Mrs. Harden
off on a stretcher.
Now Dad is in the driveway
asking what happened.
Neighbors mill around
shaking their heads,
whispering.
Mrs. Capra pats Parker
on the head.
"So you're the little hero."

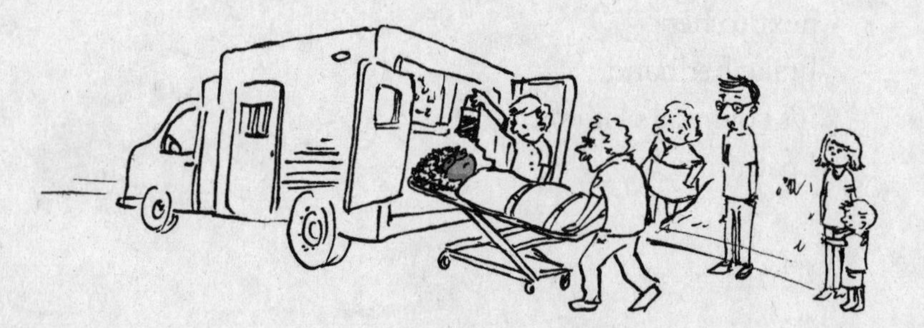

CALLING PAUL

Dad calls Mrs. Harden's nephew, Paul.
Mrs. Harden is a widow. No children.
A couple years ago she gave us
Paul's phone number "just in case."
Paul says for us to lock up
his aunt's house.
He asks us to hold her mail,
take in her newspapers,
keep an eye on things
until he finds out
what's what.

MONKEY-FACED

Back home,
Parker is all monkey-faced
(which is what he calls
being upset).

I give him a hug.
"Don't worry," I tell him.
"Mrs. Harden will be okay.

She's in good hands now."
(I don't tell him
how worried I am.)

Parker sniffles.
"Yes, but Mrs. Capra
called me a *little* hero.
I'm not little, Suzy.
I'm four and a half.
I'm a *big* hero."
Parker pumps
his (little) fist in the air.
"I'm Hero Boy!"

THREES

Wait till Mom finds out.
She likes Mrs. Harden
almost as much as I do.
Mom's in Arizona right now,
taking care of Grandma Fludd,
who recently had a bad fall.

Gee—two people I know
in the hospital.

My best friend, Alison,
says bad things come
in threes.

Uh-oh, I think.
What's next?

MOM FROM ARIZONA

Dad puts Mom on speakerphone
so Parker and I can hear too.
She says she hopes Mrs. Harden
will be okay.
She says she is proud of
her "big boy"
for dialing 911.
She says: "Thank you, Suzy Q,
for helping out with things."
("Things" is code
for Parker.)

She says she is trying to convince
Grandma Fludd to move
to Pennsylvania.
Up pipes Grandma Fludd:
"What? And freeze my patootie off
in the winter? Forget it!"
Parker howls,
wiggles his little behind.
"Patootie! Patootie!
Watch me shake my bootie!"

VOICE MAIL

There's a voice mail from Alison.
She sounds all breathless:
"Sooze, I heard about Mrs. Harden.
The whole town is talking.
I hope she's not dead.
Is she?
Is she?
Call me!
Right away!"

JUST IMAGINE

I call Alison.
"Tell me—quick!" she says.
I tell her: "We got a message
from Mrs. Harden's nephew.
She's going to be okay."
"Whew! What a relief,"
says Alison.
"Just imagine if she died.
You'd be neighbors
with a dead person!"

HOW WE STARTED

I was in second grade
when Herbie Sizemore
pushed me up against
the playground fence.
"Say it!" he ordered.
"It" was a bad word.
A very bad word.
The very, very worst.

"No," I told him.
I tried to push past him.
He wouldn't let me.
Suddenly a girl appeared,
bracelets jangling.
She stared Herbie
right in the nose.
"Let her go," she snarled.
I was surprised.
She was in the other
second-grade class.
We never played together.
Herbie growled: "This is
nunna your beeswax."
"I'm making it my beeswax,"
said the girl.
She pulled a sparkly pink phone
from her pocket.
"I have the state police
on speed dial."
"Yeah, right," said Herbie.
The girl punched a button.
Herbie backed off.
When he was gone,
I said: "That's a toy phone,

isn't it?"
The girl wagged her finger.
"Nunna your beeswax."
I laughed. "You rescued me."
"I'm Alison Wilmire," she said.
"I'm Suzy Quinn," I said.
We shook hands.
We've been best friends
ever since.

DIFFERENT

Which is pretty amazing
since we're so different.
Alison is curly blond wonder-hair.
I'm mousy brown ponytail.
She's pink sandals and short skirts.
I'm red Phillies cap and jeans.
She's hip-hop dance lessons.
I'm "Go, Phillies!"
She collects bracelets.
I collect rocks.
She wants to be an actress when she grows up.
I don't have a clue.

NOT DIFFERENT

Dad says Alison and I
are a perfect example of
the old saying
"Opposites attract."
Mom says
while Alison and I
may be different
on the outside,
we are a lot alike
on the inside
where it counts most.
"You both have heart,"
Mom says.
"That's the best thing
I can say about
a person."

TICKLE MONSTER

When Mom first went to Arizona,
Parker got all stubborn
about bedtime.

Dad and I tried extra bedtime stories.
Extra snacks.
New stuffed animals.
Old stuffed animals.
Blue night-light.
Glow-in-the-dark stickers.
Nothing worked—
until I came up with
Tickle Monster.
I started creeping
into Parker's bedroom
step by step,
waving Mom's feather duster.
"Here comes Tickle Monster,"
I'd say.
I only had to tickle Parker's big toe
before he would giggle and beg:
"Stop! Stop, Tickle Monster!
I'll sleep now!"
But this night
when I creep into his room,
he's all curled up
with his stuffed owl,
snoring like
a little eggbeater.

I guess it's exhausting
being a hero.

CHATTING

I'm tired too.
I get into my nightie.
I open my window wide.
There's a cool June breeze blowing.
It feels like it might rain.
I tell Ottilie—my goldfish—about
the day's excitement:
"Mrs. Harden nearly died today.
But Parker called 911.
And now she's going to be fine.
And the Phillies beat the Pirates—
even though I missed watching
the whole game on TV.
And we talked to Mom and Grandma Fludd."

Ottilie swims closer
to the glass in front of her tank.
Her tiny fish mouth sends me kisses.
I think she enjoys our nighttime chats.

OTTILIE

Alison says
Ottilie is just a goldfish
and goldfish don't know anything.
But I read about goldfish
before I got Ottilie.
Goldfish can recognize their owners.
They react to light and different colors.
I trained Ottilie to eat fish flakes
from my fingers.
Ottilie knows plenty.

DISGUSTING TRIVIA

Dad—who teaches history
at Ridgley Community College—
told me that in 1939
a fad was started by
a Harvard University student
who swallowed a live goldfish.
The fad spread to other colleges.
Eventually, Dad said,
the president of Boston's Animal League

decreed that goldfish swallowers
should be—would be—
arrested
if they didn't stop this behavior.
My sentiments exactly.
Ottilie's too!

GILBERT LENHARDT

This morning Gilbert Lenhardt stops by.
He heard about Mrs. Harden.
He was supposed to weed her herb garden
and pull out a dead holly bush.
He is wondering if he should go ahead.
Dad tells him yes.
Gilbert does a lot of odd jobs around the
neighborhood.
He's thirteen. Not old enough to get a
regular job.
According to Alison, Gilbert really needs
the money.
His dad drinks a lot and probably spends
his money on beer instead of his family.

For a kid with a father like that, Gilbert
is always
cheery. Always whistling.
You can hear him a block away.
Dad says they are songs from the 1940s.
Odd—but nice too.
One thing I've learned from Dad is
to appreciate ancient history.

KNOCK AT THE DOOR

Ten minutes later,
there's a knock at the door.
"Hi," says a lady in a gray suit.
"I'm Marsha Levine, reporter for
the *Ridgley Post*."
She introduces the man next to her—
"And this is Joe Perchek, photographer.
We're here to see the little boy
who called 911 yesterday.
The little hero."

NOT LITTLE

Dad says it's okay
for them to talk to Parker
for a few minutes.
And to take a couple
pictures for the paper.
Parker says: "Wait!"
He runs upstairs,
comes back wearing
his Superman T-shirt
and his Count Dracula cape
from last Halloween.
He poses—arms out
like he's flying.
Ms. Levine tweaks his cheek.
"You're the cutest little boy ever."
Parker squawks: "Don't call me little!"

PASSING MRS. BAGWELL'S

I head over to Alison's.
I pass Mrs. Bagwell's.

Mrs. Bagwell is chasing after something
with her big green flyswatter.
Mrs. Bagwell is always after something—
kids trying to retrieve balls from her yard,
beetles nibbling her roses,
the Kims' gray cat, Shady.
This time it's a crow.
I wave. "Good morning, Mrs. Bagwell."
"Dang crow," she growls.

GARNET OR CHARM?

When I get to Alison's,
she is still getting dressed.
She dangles two bracelets under my nose.

“Which one, Sooze—garnet or charm?”
I groan. “Who cares? We’re just going
to the library.”
She rolls her eyes at me. “I repeat—garnet
or charm?”
I point to the garnet bracelet.
She scowls. “You’re only saying that because
it’s red.
Like the Phillies.”
She flips both bracelets into her jewelry box.
She pulls out a purple beaded one
that matches her nails.

WHAT’S WRONG WITH READING?

I coaxed Alison into
signing up with me for
Tween Time at the Ridgley Library.
Every Tuesday morning at eleven.
She fought it.
She said she reads enough
during the school year.

I told her: "Tween Time isn't
just about reading.
It's crafts too. And games. And field trips."
Anyway—what's wrong with reading?
I happen to love it.
It's in my DNA.
I get it from my mom,
who is totally addicted to books.

MOM'S BOOK ADDICTION

Nobody—
I mean *nobody*—
loves books
more than Mom.
She breathes books—literally.
She holds them up to her nose,
takes deep whiffs.
"Each book has a scent
all its own," she says.
"Ink, tree bark, a hint of thyme,
summer-dust."
Dad pipes up: "Mold!"

He's remembering when Mom
bought six cartons of books
from someone's half-flooded basement.

Mom sleeps books.
She keeps one under her pillow.
I'm not kidding.
She got into the habit
when she was a kid.
She used to wake up at night
and read by moonlight.
I won't be shocked
if one morning
I come down to breakfast
and find Mom
in one of her fogs,
eating a page of a book
with a dollop of strawberry jam.

MEET AND GREET

We tweens, ages ten to twelve,
meet in the Bennett Room
of the Ridgley Library.

One of the librarians—Ms. Mott—
stands in the doorway.
She's wearing a black bonnet
and a fringed blue shawl.
She's twirling a parasol
(which is an umbrella for sun).
"Welcome, tweens," she says,
chirpy as a bird.
Alison gives me a dark look.
"Give it a chance," I whisper.

THEME

There are three other
kids in the room.
Two girls and a boy.
Alison and I don't know them.
Ms. Mott sighs.
She looks at her watch.
Sighs again.
I think she was hoping for
a bigger crowd.
Finally she closes her parasol.
She smiles

and makes an announcement:
"The theme for Tween Time
this summer is
everyday life in the 1800s."
Alison slumps in her seat,
hisses at me:
"I hate history!"

Q AND A

"Any questions?" asks Ms. Mott.
No one raises a hand.
I feel bad for her.
So I raise my hand.
"Yes, Suzy?"
"Was there baseball back then?"
Ms. Mott brightens. "Indeed there was.
But the field was smaller.
And players didn't wear gloves.
And batters were called strikers.
And runs were called aces."
The boy raises his hand.
"Were there cars?"
"Yes," says Ms. Mott.

“As a matter of fact, in 1895
there was a total of four cars
in the entire country.”
“Holy cow!” says the boy.
The girl in green asks,
“What did kids do for fun?”
“Simple things,” says Ms. Mott.
“Roller-skating, kite flying,
sledding, checkers, kickball,
hoop rolling.”
“What’s hoop rolling?” asks
the girl with the pigtails.
“You’ll see,” says Ms. Mott.
“We’ll be trying some of these things
in the weeks to come.”
Alison mutters under her breath:
“Whoop-dee-doo.”

SOME PUMPKINS

By the time we are dismissed,
we’ve learned quite a bit
about the 1800s.
We know that—according to

stagecoach etiquette—
it was considered bad manners
to point out where horrible murders
had been committed.
We know that
some people in the 1800s
made toothpaste out of
honey and pulverized charcoal.
And that tomatoes were
thought to be poisonous.

And that "some pumpkins"
meant "impressive"
or "very good at."

As we left, Ms. Mott chirped:
"When it comes to paying attention,
you kids are some pumpkins."

Alison grabs my arm.
"Let's skedaddle," she says—
which in 1800s talk means
"Let's get the heck out of here!"

LUNCH

Dad makes grilled cheese for lunch.
I tell him about the Tween Time theme.
Of course he's pleased.
He waves his sandwich at me.
He says what I've heard
a hundred times before:
"History is life. Its purpose is a better world."
"I *know*, Dad," I say.
Parker pipes up: "I know something too!"
"What?"
"Mrs. Bagwell got robbed!"

THE THIRD BAD THING

"You missed it, Suzy," says Parker.
"Cops came and everything."
"Only one police officer," says Dad.
"Seems Mrs. Bagwell wanted to report
a stolen ring."
"There's robbers in town!" says Parker.
"We don't know that," says Dad.

I get to thinking about
bad things happening in threes.
Grandma Fludd falls.
Mrs. Harden has a spell.
And now
Mrs. Bagwell is a crime victim.

Maybe Alison was right.

BIKES ACCORDING TO ALISON

After lunch, I get on my bike.
Alison gave hers away last year.
"Bikes are for babies," she told me
at the time.
"Tell that to Mr. Capra," I said.
"He rides his bike to work every day."
She ran her nose up the flagpole.
"Okay—babies and old people."

INTO THE BREEZE

It's a bright afternoon.
I ride my bike
into the warm breeze,
away from the house,
along the bike path.
Trees ripple green.
The light is golden.
The sky is blue.
And I am a bird
flying . . .
flying . . .
Alison doesn't know
what she's missing.

ROBBERS

I get back in time
to keep an eye on Parker
while Dad grades papers.

I set up Candy Land,
Parker's favorite board game.
Parker keeps talking about
Mrs. Bagwell's stolen ring.

Then he asks:
"Do robbers smoke?"
"What do you care?" I say.
"Just answer."
"I guess some do."

"Well, if we get a robber,
I hope he smokes."
"How come?"
"So he'll set off the smoke alarm."

BIG HERO

Parker is famous.
His photo—in his Superman shirt
and Count Dracula cape—
is on the front page of
the *Ridgley Post*.
The headline reads
LITTLE HERO DIALS 911.
Parker asks me to read it to him.
"Big Hero Dials 911,"
I say.

OBNOXIOUS

By late afternoon,
our living room is filled with
balloons,
cookie bouquets,
stuffed animals,
and flower arrangements.
All for Parker,
who is becoming
more obnoxious by the minute.

"Stay away from my balloons!"
"Don't touch my cookies!"
"Hands off my animals!"
"Don't smell my flowers!"

Little hero?
How about little monster?

RING, RING, RING

The phone doesn't stop ringing.
Mom calls.
She tells Dad to pop a copy
of the *Ridgley Post* in the mail
care of Grandma Fludd—
"Today!"

Mrs. Capra calls
to say she saw the article.
"Isn't it just wonderful!"

Alison calls.
"How does it feel?"
she asks.
"How does what feel?"
I say.
"Your brother's a hero."
"Yeah—hero brat."

The mayor's secretary calls.
She tells Dad:
"Mayor Paloma would like
your son to ride in her car
in the Fourth of July parade."

I tell Dad: "I'm going
over to the creek
to look for rocks."

No phones at the creek.

ROCK

The creek isn't far.
I leave my bike home
and walk.
I carry an old toy beach pail.
I'm fussier about my rocks
than I used to be.
I know I won't fill the pail.
I'll be happy if I find
just one special rock.
I'm ankle-deep in water
when I finally see one.
Smooth. Speckled green.
Like the egg of a rare bird.
I can feel myself smiling
as I pick it up.
Sometimes I put one of my rocks
in Ottilie's tank.
Some rocks I let Parker borrow
for when he plays with
his plastic cowboys.
Not this one.
This is one of the all-time

beauties.
This baby is all mine.

DID YOU HEAR?

"Did you find one?"
I turn. It's Alison.
"Your dad told me
you were here."
"Look," I say, all excited.
I show her the green speckled rock.
She ignores it. "Did you
hear the news?" she asks.
"Do you see my gorgeous rock?"
I ask.
Alison gives me a look.
"It's a rock," she says.
I give up.
"Yes, I heard the news.
Parker's invited
to ride in the mayor's car
in the Fourth of July parade."
"Wow!" Alison squeals.

“That’s really something. But
it’s not the news
I’m talking about.”

ALISON’S NEWS

There seems to be
a rumor going around
that Gilbert
is the one
who robbed Mrs. Bagwell,
took her ring.
Mrs. Bagwell says
she’s 95 percent certain of it.

WHERE’S THE PROOF?

Dad says Mrs. Bagwell
shouldn’t be accusing Gilbert
without proof.

Just because
Gilbert moved some boxes

from Mrs. Bagwell's attic
and had to pass by
her bedroom
where she keeps her jewelry
doesn't mean he took her ring.
"No more than I took it,"
says Dad, "when I fixed
her ceiling fan."

NICE

Mrs. Harden is being discharged
from the hospital tomorrow.
I'm making a Welcome Home card
for her.
Parker wants to make one too.
He comes into my room
with his can of broken crayons
in one hand
and a fistful of cookies
in the other.
He's still wearing
his hero outfit.
(He even sleeps in it.)

"Can you help me, Suzy?"
I give him a look. "Can you be nice?"
"I can be nice," he says.
He holds out his fist.
"Here. Take a cookie."

STAYING WITH MRS. HARDEN

Mrs. Harden is home and
looking tired.
Her nephew, Paul,
has an important meeting today.
He asks if I will stay
with his aunt
for a couple hours—
"just to make sure
there are no problems."
"Sure," I tell him.
And it's a good thing
I'm there,
because as soon as Mrs. Harden
goes up to her room
to take a nap,
the doorbell starts ringing.

It's the mailman
with a package.

It's the florist
with a dozen roses.

It's Mrs. Capra
with a bowl of stewed plums.
And then Mrs. Kim
with cookies.

Last, it's Mrs. Bagwell
with one of those
rotisserie chickens
from the supermarket.

I don't like how
Mrs. Bagwell is blaming
Gilbert
for stealing her ring
when she has no proof.

I act polite, though.
I tell her Mrs. Harden
is resting.
I thank her for the chicken.

I feel like throwing the chicken
into the garbage.
But I don't.
The chicken didn't
accuse Gilbert.

THE DOORBELL AGAIN

Mrs. Harden is up from her nap
when the doorbell rings again.
It's Gilbert.
He's carrying a big planter of mint.
"Keep it in the pot," he says,

sounding like a garden pro.
"If you plant it in the ground,
it will take over."

Mrs. Harden smiles.
"I'll set it on the patio tomorrow,"
she says. "For now, put it on
the coffee table
so I can smell it."

I'm careful not to mention
Mrs. Bagwell's accusation.
For a while I think Gilbert
is doing okay until I realize
I didn't hear him whistling
up the walk.

SOMEDAY

I walk out with Gilbert
to the end of the driveway.
I want to say something
that will cheer him up.
"So, Gilbert. Want to do something?"

"Sure. But you're busy now."
"Right—so . . . someday?"
"Okay. Good. Someday.
Do what?"
"Right. What?"
"Well?"
"Want to collect rocks with me?"
Gilbert frowns.
"Scratch rock collecting," I say.
"No offense," he says. "I'm just
not into rocks."
"I understand," I say. "So . . . let's think.
What do we both like?"
"How about food?" he says.
"Food—" I say. "Can't go wrong
with that."
"Ice cream," he says.
I give him a high five. "Ice cream!"
"Someday," he says.
"Someday," I say. I head back
to Mrs. Harden.
Suddenly I turn and call to Gilbert:
"My treat!"
Gilbert gives a fist pump.
"Yes!"

HAPPY NEWS

Mom is coming home!
On Saturday.
Grandma Fludd is much stronger.
And she has lots of friends
at Sunshine Terrace
if she needs anything.
I didn't realize how much
I missed Mom
until I burst into tears
when Dad told me.

SHIRT

It takes a lot of convincing,
but finally I get Parker
to accept the fact
that he can be a hero
without the Superman shirt.

I tell him it's starting to stink.
I tell him the bad guys
will smell him coming.

He lets me pull the shirt off.
He puts on the Phillies shirt
I got him last Christmas.

I can't talk him out of
the cape.

JUST A FRIEND

Alison stops by.
I tell her I'm going to Bean's Books.
"Mom is flying home on Saturday.
I want to get her a gift card."
Alison says she'll come along.

On the way
Alison brings up Gilbert
and Mrs. Bagwell's ring.
I tell her: "I don't want to talk about it."
"Why not?"
"It's gossip and Gilbert is a friend."
Alison raises an eyebrow. "Aha!"
"A *friend*."
"A *boy*friend," she squeals. "Wooo-hoooo."

I poke her. “Back off. He’s just a friend.
Who happens to be a boy.”
“Well, anyway,” says Alison. “My cousin Tara
says he probably did it.
Where there’s smoke, there’s fire.”

“That’s it,” I say. “I’m not going to
talk about it.”

Alison clamps her lips together. “Fine,” she says.
“Fine,” I say.

MOOD CHANGE

One thing about Alison—
she doesn’t stay in the same mood
for long.
By the time we get to Bean’s,

she's back to being chatty.
"So," she says, "what do you want
for your birthday?"
"Well, there's no point asking for
my own phone or computer," I say.
"Dad already told me. Not till I'm thirteen."
Alison's parents have told her the same thing.
She rolls her eyes. "Parents!"

MY BIRTHDAY UPCOMING

My birthday is July 15.
I'll be twelve.
I've been calling myself twelve
since school let out.
Mom says not to wish my childhood away.
But I don't think of myself
as a child.
Parker is a child. I'm a kid.
There's a difference.
I've already told my parents
what I want for my twelfth birthday.
I want to go to a Phillies game.

EXPENSIVE

Citizens Bank Park—
home to the Philadelphia Phillies—
is a two-and-a-half-hour drive
from Ridgley.
Going to a game
means staying over
at a hotel in the city.
So it would be
an expensive
birthday present.
But hey—it's the big one-two.
A person turns twelve
only once.

CHAT WITH OTTILIE

I tell Ottilie:
"Mrs. Harden is out of the hospital."
Ottilie flicks her tail fin.
I think it's her way of smiling.
"And Mom is coming home.
And I forgot to tell you before—

Parker is riding with Mayor Paloma
in the Fourth of July parade."
Another fin flick.
"And I'm jealous and—"
The fin stops.
I stop.
My hand shoots to my mouth,
clamps it shut.
Ottilie and I boggle at each other,
both fish-eyed.
I can't believe I said that.

FRIDAY-MORNING VISIT

I go over to check on Mrs. Harden.
She is up and dressed
and having tea.
Her cheeks are rosy.

She doesn't look tired anymore.
She gives me a hug.
"I'm so glad you stopped by, Suzy,"
she says.
"I have something for Parker."

PRESENTS

Mrs. Harden goes into the hall.
She returns with a teddy bear
dressed like a doctor,
complete with a tiny stethoscope.
"I got it at the hospital gift shop.
Think Parker will like it?"
"Sure," I say.
Then she hands me a box
tied with red ribbon.
"And this is for you, Suzy."
"Me?" I say.
"I'm not the one who called 911."
Mrs. Harden drapes an arm around me.
"No, but I have a nice, fuzzy memory
of you holding my hand.
I can still hear you saying,

'Don't worry, Mrs. Harden.
Help is on the way.'"

TEARS AGAIN

I untie the ribbon
and open the box.
And for the second time
in two days,
I burst into tears.
There, nestled in tissue paper,
is a foot-long memento baseball bat.
It says
PHILLIES WORLD CHAMPIONS
2008.
Mrs. Harden grins.
"I was going to give it to you
for your birthday."
I hug the bat to my chest.
"This is birthday and Easter
and Christmas
for the rest of my life!"

READ ALOUD

Later,
Alison and I are sitting
on the front porch.
I'm reading to her
the first chapter of
Black Beauty,
which Ms. Mott recommended to me
since it was written in the 1800s.
Reading aloud is one way
I try to get Alison into a book.

Alison inspects her nails,
flaps at a fly,
yawns.
"I'm bored," she says.
I give a sigh.
"How can you be bored?
I just started. Besides,
don't you want to be an actress?"

Alison shrugs. "Yeah—so?"
"So actresses have to read scripts."

She snorts. "I know that.
When I was in the school play,
I not only read the whole play—
I memorized it."
"I rest my case," I say. "You do read."
"Only plays I'm in."
"Just let me finish this chapter."
Alison gives me a wicked grin.
"Can't. Here comes Gilbert,
your not-boyfriend."

NOT FOR ME

Gilbert isn't here for me.
"Is your dad around?"
he asks.
"Mr. Kim's lawn mower
won't start.
I can't figure out
what's wrong."

LAWN-MOWER MAN

Dad loves tinkering
with lawn mowers.
There are four in our garage.
Only one works.
The others Dad got at yard sales.
They don't run now, but they will.
And once they work,
he'll give them away
and buy more.
Mom calls it
Dad's "harmless addiction."
Like hers with books.

DON'T ASK ME

Dad has worked on
Mr. Kim's lawn mower before.
Mr. Kim, who recently retired
from NASA,
always jokes with Dad.

He says: "I can send a man
to the moon, but don't ask me
to fix a lawn mower."

NICE WATCH

Dad comes out to the front porch.
Parker too.
Gilbert gives Parker a friendly punch
on the arm.
"Nice cape, buddy," he says.
Parker eyeballs Gilbert's watch.
"Nice watch."
"Thanks. I got it at Trader Bill's."
Parker lowers his voice to a whisper.
"Be careful with that watch.
There's robbers in town."

JUST GETTING STARTED

Alison shoots me a look.
I ignore her.
Gilbert tilts his head,

reads my book title.
"*Black Beauty*, huh?
Any good?"
"Just getting started," I say.
"Well, you can tell me
how you like it
over ice cream,"
he says.
He winks at me.
"Someday."
Alison jabs me
with her elbow,
hisses under her breath:
"Aha!"

AFTER SUPPER

I decide to clean the kitchen
for when Mom comes home.
Dad's great with lawn mowers
and grilled cheese sandwiches
and history
and lots of other stuff.
But cleaning—forget it.

Parker wants to help.
He stands on a chair
to wash Dad's coffee mug
and topples over.
Next he drops the sugar bowl.
Then he steps on my foot.
"Time to go play," I tell him.
He stomps off.
"Play, play, play—that's all I do."
A familiar voice replies:
"What a tragic life you have, Parky."

SURPRISE

I scream—
"Mom!"
I race into the hall.
I throw my arms around Mom's neck.
"I thought you weren't coming home
until tomorrow night."
Mom tucks a strand of hair
behind my ear.
"Oh, sweetie, I missed you all so much."

PANCAKES

Early Saturday morning
Dad calls:
"Who wants to
go to the Pancake Palace?"
My eyes pop open.
Chocolate chip pancakes—
one of the best foods
ever invented.
I'm dressed and ready to go
in two minutes.

FAMOUS FAR AND WIDE

The waitress hands us our menus.
They're so big that Parker—
who can't read but pretends he can—
totally disappears behind his.
But not before the waitress says:
"Hey—aren't you the little boy
who called 911?
The little hero?"

MORE PRESENTS

Grandma Fludd has sent gifts
home with Mom:
A fountain pen for Dad.
(He uses ballpoint.)
A box of cactus candy for Parker.
(He takes one bite and spits it out.)
And for me—
oh no—
a pair of earrings.
Clip-ons
shaped like saguaros.
I roll my eyes.
Mom tells me: "Sit tight.
I'll be right back."

MOM'S OWN STASH

Mom comes back
with a cardboard box.
She pulls stuff out:
A Tommy Tool screwdriver.
A pair of brown mittens

as wide as waffles.
A fan with the logo
of Frawley's Funeral Parlor
on the front.
A pin in the shape of a crab.
A pair of ballet slippers.
I gape. "I didn't know you took ballet."
Mom laughs. "I didn't."
"Then what—"
Suddenly it dawns on me.
"Grandma Fludd gave you
this junk," I say.
Mom shakes her head.
"Not Grandma Fludd.
And absolutely
not junk."

ANOTHER GRANDMA

Mom tells me about Grandma O'Dell.
Grandma O'Dell was Grandma Fludd's
mother—
and therefore my mom's grandmother.
My great-grandmother.

"She was wonderful," Mom says.
"She took me to afternoon tea
at fancy hotels.
We both wore hats and gloves.
She taught me Broadway show tunes.
She took me to New York City twice
on the train.
But, oh my, she gave the oddest presents."
"Must run in the family," I say.
"I threw a lot of the stuff away," Mom says.
"But some I dumped in this box."

"I don't blame you."
"Then last week Grandma Fludd found the box
in her storage bin and gave it to me."
"How come you didn't ditch it at the airport?"
Mom's eyes get shiny.
"Because you don't ditch your treasures."

TREASURE

Mom tells me she would give anything
"to be having tea with Grandma O'Dell again,
opening odd little gifts:
a Daffy Duck change purse,
a pig made of tiny seashells . . ."
I interrupt:
"A pair of clip-on earrings
shaped like saguaros?"

AFTER MOM LEAVES

I take my black dress shoes
(which I hardly ever wear)
out of their box.

I line the box with tissue paper.
I put the clip-ons in the box.
Also the comb shaped like an alligator
that Grandma Fludd sent me for Easter.
And the plastic jelly beans.
"This is my treasure box,"
I tell Ottilie.
"From my grandmother."
Ottilie swims to the surface,
puckers her mouth.
That's Ottilie-speak for
"Where's my fish flakes?"

CROWS

After church on Sunday,
Mrs. Harden invites me over
to work on her 1,000-piece puzzle.
She's got a card table
set up in her living room.
Puzzle pieces lie in heaps
in each corner.
"You work that side, Suzy,"
she tells me.

The picture on the puzzle box
is of three crows
sitting on a clothesline.
I tell Mrs. Harden how
Mrs. Bagwell chased after
that crow with her flyswatter.
Mrs. Harden says: "Lucky for her
that crow didn't swoop down
and land on her head."
Now that's a puzzle picture
I'd like to work on!

TAKING A BREAK

An hour is about all we can take
of puzzle-making.
We stop for lemonade.
Mrs. Harden asks about Grandma Fludd.
I tell her Grandma Fludd is doing fine.
I tell her about the saguaro earrings
and my new treasure box.
Mrs. Harden grabs my hand.
"I have a treasure box too.
Come see!"

MRS. HARDEN'S TREASURE BOX

Mrs. Harden's treasure box is not a box at all.
It's a small trunk in her spare room,
and it's filled:
Her own baby quilt, hand-stitched by an aunt.
A Little Lulu doll.
Three packets of letters tied with string.
A stack of report cards.
(Mrs. Harden was a straight-A student.
I'm straight B—except for my A in English.)
A navy blue sweater Mrs. Harden knitted
for her husband on their first anniversary.
The wooden bird I painted for her when
I was six.

Her father's old deflated football.
A white dress with a lace collar.
"Is that your wedding dress?" I ask.
"No," says Mrs. Harden. "I was married
in a gray suit. This dress belonged to
my mother. She wore it to her
high school graduation."
"It's very pretty," I say—even though
I'm not a fan of dresses.
I can't remember the last time I wore one.

TANTRUM

Mom works for Dr. Ellis,
former dean of Ridgley Community College.
She's his part-time personal assistant.
This morning she's about to go over to
his house.
Parker whines to go along.
Sometimes Mom takes him.
Dr. Ellis lets Parker build forts and firehouses
with his many hundreds of books
as long as Parker promises
to be careful with each one.

Dr. Ellis says that's how he came
to love books,
by building walls and castles
with his own father's collection.
Mom tells Parker: "Not today."
Parker flops onto the floor.
He rolls.
He kicks his feet in the air
like a bug.
He shrieks.
Until I say:
"What kind of superhero does that?"

HEY

Later, Parker's friend Franky
invites Parker over to play.
Dad has a class to prepare.
Mrs. Harden is off to
her doctor's appointment.
Alison is at her hip-hop lesson.
I decide to wash my bike.
Gilbert walks past.

I call out: "Hey, Gilbert."
"Hey, Suzy."
I want to tell Gilbert
I don't believe for one second
that he took Mrs. Bagwell's ring.
I want to tell him I miss the whistling.
I want to tell him I snipped some
of the mint he gave to Mrs. Harden
and am rooting it in a jar
on my windowsill.
But ever since Alison
made a joke about me liking Gilbert
as a boyfriend,
I've gotten a little shy around him.
And neither of us has mentioned
ice cream lately.

EGG SALAD'S IN THE FRIDGE

When Mom comes home from Dr. Ellis's,
I tell her I'll need a bag lunch
for Tween Time tomorrow.
She tells me there's egg salad in the fridge.

Of course I can make my own lunch.
My dinner too.
But Mom was in Arizona for weeks,
and I'm kind of in the mood
for a little pampering.

Then Parker hops onto Mom's lap.
"I want Smileys," he says.
Smileys are oatmeal cookies
with happy raisin faces.
"I'll make some tonight,"
Mom tells him.

"Anything for the little hero,"
I say under my breath.

TWEEN TIME SURPRISE

The Tween Time plan for the day
is a "surprise" field trip.
Alison and I bring permission slips
and bag lunches.
Ms. Mott collects our lunches

in a big wicker basket.
She jabs at the air with
her closed parasol.
"Off we go," she says,
still not telling us where we're going.
Alison groans. "It's a picnic.
I hate picnics. All those bugs."
"It'll be fun," I say.
The boy asks Ms. Mott:
"Where are we going?"
"To Old Elm Cemetery," Ms. Mott says.
Alison hisses in my ear. "Cemetery? *Fun?*
Did you say fun?"
I say: "Okay . . . interesting."

SOME CAME FOR THE QUIET

Old Elm Cemetery
is a fifteen-minute walk
from the library.
Dad has talked about it,
but I've never been there
till now.

It's pretty, really.
Old trees.
Tall hedges.
Flowering bushes.
Mossy marble stones.

Ms. Mott spreads
a red-checkered tablecloth.
We sit in a circle
eating our lunches.
Alison swats a bee
from her cupcake.

Ms. Mott tells us
how people in the 1800s
used to picnic here,
because there weren't
many open spaces
for the public back then.
A cemetery was like a park.

She says: "Some people came
just to be near loved ones
who had died.

They found it comforting.
Some people came
just for the quiet."

Suddenly
Alison shrieks:
"Holy tamales!
I think
I just bit into a bug!"

THE PAIN

On the way home,
Alison hooks her arm
into mine.
"I know I'm a pain."
I don't say anything.
"A first-rate complainer.
Don't deny it, Sooze."
I don't deny it.
"It's in my DNA.
Blame my aunt Gertrude."
Silence.

Alison turns, gives me
a big hug.
Right there
on the sidewalk.
"Thanks for putting up
with me," she says.

You gotta love her!

JUST US SOMEDAY

Dad asks if we tweens
walked around the cemetery,
if we looked at headstones.
"No," I say. "We just had a picnic."

Dad says: "Maybe you and I
can go for a walk around Old Elm
someday. Check out
the headstones."
The part about
looking at headstones
sounds pretty depressing.
But I do like the part about

me and Dad doing something
together.
Just us two.
Without
the little hero.

GINGERBREAD

On Wednesday morning,
Mrs. Harden calls
to see if I want to
help her make
a gingerbread cake
for Gilbert.
Today is his birthday,
and gingerbread
is his favorite.

HOW IT'S DONE

Mrs. Harden measures the flour.
I crack eggs,
pour molasses.

Ginger
and cloves
and cinnamon
go into the bowl.
I used to like licking the bowl
until Alison told me
raw batter
can kill you.

A CARD FOR GILBERT

While the cake is baking,
I make Gilbert a card.
Red and white

with baseball stickers,
because Gilbert likes the Phillies
almost as much as I do.
I print HAPPY BIRTHDAY inside—
though how happy can it be
with a dad who drinks too much
and a neighbor who thinks
you are a thief.

PERFECT

The cake is finished.
Mrs. Harden dusts it
with powdered sugar.
She puts it in her cake carrier.
She asks me to bring
Gilbert's present along.
It's a Phillies T-shirt
in a Phillies backpack,
and doesn't the card
I made for Gilbert
go perfectly.

WHERE GILBERT LIVES

I'd never been to Gilbert's house.
We drive ten blocks.
I expected a small house—
maybe with Gilbert's dad
drinking beer and slouching
on an old lawn chair.
But there's no sign of
Gilbert's dad.
As for the house,
I was right.
It *is* small.
But there's something
I didn't expect:
it's also very
pretty.

TELLING OTTILIE

I tell Ottilie
about Gilbert's house.
About the blue shutters

and window boxes
dripping pink petunias.

I tell Ottilie
about the wind chimes
twinkling.
The brick patio
Gilbert built himself
with bricks from
the old print shop.

I tell Ottilie
how Gilbert's mom
brought us iced tea
with fresh mint
from her herb garden.
And how she served the cake
on flowered plates—
so what if they didn't match.

I tell Ottilie
how glad I am
that Gilbert's life
isn't just about
his dad's drinking.

Or not having much money.
Or Mrs. Bagwell
saying bad things about him.
It's also about his nice mom.
His pretty house.
And his friends sharing
homemade birthday cake
on a patio he built himself.

I DON'T TELL OTTILIE

That I find myself
thinking about
Gilbert.
A lot.
Like a big brother?
I ask myself.
Not really.
How about a cousin?
Nope.
Or a special friend?
Getting close.
A *very* special friend?
BINGO!

THE FIRST DAY OF JULY

All of a sudden
everyone is thinking about
Ridgley's Fourth of July parade—
which will be on July 3 this year
because the Fourth falls on a Sunday.

Mr. Capra says
he and the people he works with
are putting together a bike brigade—
streamers and flags,
fancy baskets and bells.

Mr. Kim is refurbishing
his float from last year,
patching the rocket with aluminum foil,
blowing up another yellow beach-ball moon,
repainting the clay astronauts.

Ridgley High's marching band
is practicing on the football field.

Mr. Ellis has Mom dust off
his George Washington costume.

Alison and I are signed up
to walk with the Ridgley Library group.
We'll wear T-shirts that read
I LUV MY LIBRARY.

And Parker,
the little hero,
gets to ride in Mayor Paloma's
cool blue convertible
with the top down.

TAKING PARKER'S CAPE

Mom tries to take Parker's ratty old cape.
Parker clutches it around his neck.
He howls.
"You don't need a cape
to be a hero," Dad tells him.
More howling.
"It's ripped," I say. "And it smells yucky."
Parker holds his nose.
"*You* smell yucky, Suzy Poo-poo," he says.
Mom wheedles. "Now, Parky, what if we get you

a new cape? Something really nice for the
parade?"
Parker stops clutching. He sniffles.
"Will it have blue stars?"
Mom nods. "If you want blue stars."
"When?" he asks.
"In a couple days."
"Okay," he says. "But I'm wearing
this one till then."
Later, Mom sneaks it off him
when he's sleeping.
She throws it in the trash can.

HAPPY

Mom gets Mrs. Capra—
a master quilter—
to make the new cape.
"Lots of stars!" says Parker.
"You got it," says Mrs. Capra.

Next Parker decides he wants
a haircut.
Dad takes him to the barbershop.

Then Mayor Paloma's assistant calls
with instructions:
"Bring the boy to the mayor's office
at nine a.m. sharp on the day
of the parade."

The parade doesn't start till ten,
but there's going to be
a brief ceremony first.
Parker will get a medal.
There will be photos with the mayor.

It seems as though
the whole parade
is about Parker.
Oh well—my birthday
is coming up,
and Dad is going to take me
to a Phillies game.
Good seats . . . hot dogs . . .
root beer . . . rally towel . . .
maybe even an autograph
or two.
On July 15.

At least I'll be a star
that day.

STORM

I'm walking home from Alison's.
She wanted us to make fancy headbands
to wear in the parade tomorrow.
Suddenly the sky goes dark.
Lightning flashes.
Fat drops of rain fall.
I start to run.
Old newspapers fly past.
A trash-can lid clatters by.
Now it's pouring, and I'm soaked.
I can't see ahead.
Through the howling wind, I hear my name.
I move toward the voice—
It's Mrs. Bagwell standing at her door.
"Hurry, Suzy! Come inside!"
I make it to her doorway.
Then the whole earth shakes.
My ears pop, and it feels like

the end of the world
as Mrs. Bagwell and I leap
into her hall closet
together.

NOT THE END OF THE WORLD

It was not the end of the world.
It was the sixty-five-foot evergreen
in Mrs. Bagwell's backyard
uprooting and crashing down
just inches from the house.

It was not the end of the world,
but it could have been
for me and Mrs. Bagwell
if the angle of the tree-fall
had been the least bit different.

It could have been
the end.

GILBERT COMES BY

"I heard about the tree," he says.
"Are you okay?"
I give him a thumbs-up.
"Thanks to your friend Mrs. Bagwell."
"So I guess it's true." He smiles. "There's
good in everyone."
"Where were *you* in the storm?" I ask.
"At home," he says. "Eating ice cream."
We both laugh.
We sit there on the porch
just talking,
being.
The trees glisten green.
I've never seen
trees so green.

JULY 3

Parker is so wound up
before the parade
that he throws up

his cornflakes.
Twice.

Mom is so excited
about meeting the mayor
that she heads out the door
with two different shoes on.

Alison does my hair
with the fancy hairband.
She keeps saying:
"I can't believe it! You were
almost crushed to death!
By a Christmas tree!"

A zillion people
drive past Mrs. Bagwell's
famous fallen evergreen.
Some try to take photos.

Some succeed.
Some she chases off
with her flyswatter.

The parade goes fine
except when
Uncle Sam on stilts
topples over into the crowd
and sprains his ankle.

Oh, and when Paco the Parrot
squawks a stream of
bad words.

It's an odd sort of day.
Alison blames it on the storm.
"Something's in the air," she says.
"I can smell it."
I give her a look. "I can smell it too.
You're wearing too much perfume."

THE FOURTH OF JULY

Parker wears his cape
and his medal from the mayor
to church.
Pastor McCleary actually mentions
Parker in his sermon.

All day Parker flashes the medal
in our faces.
He even goes into my room
to show off
to Ottilie.

At the fireworks
Parker struts around our blanket
flashing his medal,
flapping his cape.
Twice Mom tells him
to "please sit down."
But there's such a smile
in her voice
he totally ignores her.
I really don't know
how much more
of this little hero stuff
I can take.

GUESS

On Tuesday
on the way to Tween Time

Alison is all bubbly with
guess-whos
and guess-whats.

"Guess who *really* stole
Mrs. Bagwell's ring?"

"Guess what Mrs. Bagwell
is doing *now*?"

"Guess what you and I
are going to do this Friday?"

I hold my hand up. "Whoa!
One guess at a time, please."

WHO REALLY STOLE THE RING

"A crow!" Alison tells me.
She jabs her finger at me and repeats:
"A crow!"
I think Alison is getting goofy.
"Crows steal jewelry?"
"Yes!" she says. "The tree guy

found the ring in a crow's nest
when he was sawing off the branches
of Mrs. Bagwell's tree.
There it was all shiny—
couldn't miss it."
"And he gave it to Mrs. Bagwell?" I ask.
Alison grins. "Honesty is alive and well
in good old Ridgley."
"But how—?"
"Seems Mrs. Bagwell was wearing
the ring last spring.
She took it off to pick up a clump
of muddy leaves.
She set it on her patio table.
A crow must have spied it."

Of course at the bottom
of it all,
I couldn't care less about
crow, nest, or ring.
"What about poor Gilbert?" I ask.
Alison grins again.
"I'm coming to that."

ALISON COMES TO THAT

"Well," she says, "Mrs. Bagwell was
so embarrassed about accusing Gilbert
that she drove right over
to his home and apologized."
"Really?" I say.
"Really!
And she told Gilbert
to go to Ernie's Bike Shop
and choose *any* bike he likes."
I shake my head.
"Are we talking about
our Mrs. Bagwell?"
"You bet," says Alison. "And
my dad heard she is going to
put an ad in the *Ridgley Post*
that her misplaced ring
has been found."
"Sounds like Mrs. Bagwell
is a changed woman," I say.
Alison snorts. "Not totally.
Earlier, I saw her chasing
the Kims' cat with her flyswatter."

WHAT ABOUT FRIDAY?

When we get to the library,
Ms. Mott waves us through the door.
There's no time to ask Alison
about what she's planning for us
on Friday.
Just as well.
It's probably something
I'm going to hate.
Like getting our nails done.
(Alison's cousin Tara
likes to practice on us.)
Or making bracelets
with Alison's bead kit.
Or Alison trying to teach me
her latest hip-hop routine.

FAMOUS PEOPLE FROM THE 1800S

Pictures are tacked up
all around the Bennett Room,
pictures of famous people
from the 1800s.

Abraham Lincoln

Edgar Allan Poe

Harriet Tubman

Ms. Mott points to each one:
Abraham Lincoln—president of the
United States.
Florence Nightingale—nurse.
Sarah Bernhardt—actress.

Emily Dickinson

Edgar Allan Poe—author.
Harriet Tubman—"conductor" of the
Underground Railroad.
Emily Dickinson—poet.

Chief Joseph

Chief Joseph—chief of the Nez Perce Nation.
Annie Oakley—star of Buffalo Bill's Wild
West show.
Frederick Douglass—leader in the
abolitionist movement.

Annie Oakley

Ms. Mott instructs us to choose
the person we'd like to learn more about.
Alison elbows me. "Learn," she growls.
"What is this? School?"
"Shhh," I say.

Frederick Douglass

Ms. Mott goes on. "Once you've decided,
you may choose a few books from the back table
about that person."
Alison mock-cheers. "Yippee."

"And next week," says Ms. Mott, "we'll
each come
dressed as our favorite, ready to share
what we've learned.

Alison leans over and whispers: "Next week
I'm going to be sick with one of those
1800s diseases.
What were they—typhoid fever? Gout?"
But when Ms. Mott asks Alison about
her choice,
Alison replies all nice and polite:
"Sarah Bernhardt, Ms. Mott. The actress."
Ms. Mott pats Alison on the head.
"Why am I not surprised?"

MY TURN

I don't know what draws me
to Emily Dickinson.
I'm more the Annie Oakley type.
But it's something about
Emily's face—
her eyes, I think.

She looks so content.
And her hands—
so graceful and relaxed.
"I'll be Emily Dickinson,"
I tell Ms. Mott.
Ms. Mott sends me a smile.
"Good choice, Suzy."

NOT MY TYPE

I take three books
about Emily Dickinson
from the table.
When Alison goes
to the ladies' room,
I skim a few pages.
I read that Emily
had a talent
for the piano.
She called it "moosic."
As she got older,
she stopped going places.
She even hid from guests
who came to the house.

She carried on her friendships
by letter.
She wore only white dresses.

Not exactly my kind of chick.

COMPLAIN, COMPLAIN, COMPLAIN

On the way home,
all Alison does is
complain.
"No way am I going to read
an entire book
on summer vacation."
"Just skim it," I tell her.
She ignores that. Keeps whining.
"And a report!
Is Ms. Mott joking?
That's homework. Homework! In *July*!"
"You don't have to give a long report,"
I say. "Just a little something about
your person."
"Let's just quit Tween Time."
"No way," I tell her. "I like Tween Time."

Then, to change the subject, I ask:
"So—what's this about Friday?
What are you and I going to do?"
Her sour face brightens. She claps her hands.
"We're auditioning for a play!"

WANTED

The next day,
Alison and I go to
the Ridgley Community Theater.
The sign on the door says:
WANTED:
ACTORS AGES 10 TO 13
TO PERFORM IN UPCOMING PLAY
THE FOGGY BOG MURDERS.
AUDITIONS FRIDAY, JULY 9

I tell Alison: "I can't audition
for a play."
"Why not?"
"I wouldn't know what to do."
Alison drapes her arm around me.
"I'll tell you what to do."

"Besides," I say, "I don't want to
be an actress. You do."
"Maybe you do too," says Alison.
"You just don't know it yet."

PRACTICE

We go to Alison's.
Up in her room
she digs through some papers
and comes up with
the script from
last year's school play,
Snow White in the Big City.

Alison played the lead—
Snow White.
I was stage crew.

She plops on the bed
beside me.
"We'll practice with this," she says.
"I'll be Snow White."
"Of course."

"You'll be the witch."
"Of course."

SET

So it's set.
For the audition we will do
a scene from *Snow White in the Big City*.
Alison tucks her blond curls
under the old Snow White wig.
The witchiest thing she can find for me
is an old black T-shirt of her father's.
There's a hole under one arm.

WITCHES CACKLE

We sit back on the bed.
We turn pages to the part where
the witch—posing as a waitress—
tries to get Snow White to order
the poison-apple Danish.
I read my line: "This Danish is delicious.
You must try it, my dear."

Alison—as herself—screeches: “No! No! No!
You’re supposed to be a *witch*. You sound like
that nice waitress at Daisy Donuts.”
“Well, aren’t I a waitress *and* a witch?”
Alison looks at the ceiling, then back at me.
“You’re mainly a witch. You have to sound like
a witch.”
Alison demonstrates. Her voice turns sinister:
“Zees Danish eez dee-lizzious. You muuuzzt
try eet.”
She goes on: “Then you cackle. Like this—
HEE-HEE-HEE-HEE-HEE!”
“Do I *have* to cackle?” I ask.
Alison smacks her forehead.
“Yes, you have to cackle.
Witches cackle.
You’re a witch.
You *cackle*.”

NO WONDER

Dad likes that I am learning
about Emily Dickinson.
At dinner, he tells a story

about Emily's father,
Mr. Dickinson—
who left the house
in his underwear one night
and woke the entire
neighborhood
with church bells
so that the people could see
the northern lights.

"Whew!" I say.
"With a dad like that,
no wonder Emily
didn't want to
leave the house."

MORE PRACTICE

After dinner,
I practice my cackling
on Ottilie.
She hides behind
her sunken treasure chest.
Mom calls upstairs:

"Suzy Q, what's going on?
Are you laughing or crying?"
"Neither," I call down.
"I'm cackling."

THERE WAS A TIME

There was a time—
not so long ago—
when Mom was actually
interested in me
and would have walked upstairs,
poked her head in my door,
and asked me *why*
I was cackling.

Now
she stays downstairs,
all busy baking more Smileys
for Hero Boy.

BEDTIME POEM

Before bed,
I choose an Emily Dickinson poem
to read to Ottilie.
It's the one that begins:
"*Ah, Moon—and Star!*
You are very far—"
Those are the only two lines
of the poem I understand.
Ottilie swims to the other side
of her tank.
I think she agrees with me.
I tell her to do
what my English teacher,
Mr. Ranft, told us:
"When you don't understand
the words of a poem,
just let the sounds wash over you."
Easier for Ottilie since she lives
underwater.

DREAM

That night I dream
I am Emily Dickinson.
The moon is far.
The stars are twinkling.
I peek at them
through my curtain.
I am wearing a white gown.
I sit at the piano that
is in my room.
I play beautiful
“moosic.”
People from all over Ridgley
gather in the front yard.
Dad goes out on the porch
in his underwear
and thanks them for coming—
“But my daughter
doesn’t receive visitors,”
he says.

A PERFECT JULY DAY

Gilbert is in Mrs. Harden's driveway
on his new bike—
a silver Schwinn Corvette
with black trim.
I go over to admire it.
"Cool," I say.
Gilbert grins, then says:
"Want to ride bikes over to
Ridgley Park?"
"Darn," I say. "I can't.
Alison and I are going to
practice our parts."
"Parts?"
"We're auditioning for a play
together.
On Friday."
Gilbert gives me a thumbs-up.
"Good luck."
He starts to pedal away,
leaving me alone with the day,
one of those perfect July days:
breeze,
smell of fresh-cut grass,

sky blue as poster paint.
I pull out my own bike,
hop on,
pedal hard.

CATCHING UP

I catch up with Gilbert in the park.
He and his new bike are leaning against a tree.
"Hey," I say.
Gilbert looks up. "Hey, Suzy. I thought you
were going to Alison's."
"I'll go later," I tell him.
I get off my bike and sit on the grass.
Gilbert sits next to me.
"My birthday's coming up," I say.
"July fifteenth."
Gilbert grins. "Thanks for the heads-up."
I laugh. "I'm not fishing for a card or present.
I'm just saying that my dad's taking me
to a Phillies game."
As soon as the words are out of my mouth,
I regret them.
I'm pretty sure Gilbert's dad

would never take him to a game.
So I'm shocked when Gilbert tells me
his dad took him last fall—
to see the Phillies play the Atlanta Braves.
What pops in my head next is:
I thought your dad had a drinking problem.
Of course I know better than to say
everything that pops into my head.
Instead I ask: "So—did you get any autographs?"

MORE

Gilbert and I sit for a while
pulling blades of grass.

Then I tell him
how annoying it is
when your little brother
is a hero.

And Gilbert tells me
how much he misses
his best friend, Luis,
who is spending the summer
with cousins in New York.

And I tell Gilbert
how nervous I am about
trying out for the play.

And he tells me
how worried he was
that Mrs. Bagwell's ring
would never turn up.

And I tell him
how much I missed
his whistling.

And he tells me
how much he appreciated
that I never treated him
like a thief.

And we both laugh about
Mrs. Bagwell's
dreaded green flyswatter.

And then we just sit there
on the grass
not saying much of anything.

BEING LATE

When I finally get to Alison's,
she is hopping mad.
"Where the heck were you?" she growls.
"Riding my bike," I tell her. "Talking
to Gilbert."
Alison shoots me a glare.
"I knew it!"
"Big deal," I say. "I'm only ten minutes late."
"Ha!" Alison snorts. "Tell that to
the director on Friday."
"I won't be late on Friday."
"Well, if you are," she says, "you can
kiss this friendship goodbye."
I give one of Alison's curls a tug.

"I said I won't be late."
"Fine," she says.
"Fine," I say.

READY

Alison and I practice our lines.
I try two kinds of cackling.
"Go with the first cackle,"
Alison tells me.
Then she takes a fake bite
of the fake Danish
and fake faints
while I cackle—
over and over
and over again.
Finally
she pronounces us
ready for the audition.
She tells me to go home,
eat protein for dinner,
and get a good night's sleep.
"Rest my cackle," I say.
She almost grins.

THURSDAY SUPPER

Mom is in one of her fogs
this afternoon.
She started looking up a recipe
for spinach ravioli
and ended up reading
half the cookbook.
So it's plain cheese omelets
for supper.
Protein.
Alison will be pleased.

ANNOUNCEMENT

I make my announcement
over dessert.
"I'm going to audition tomorrow."
Mom's spooned rice pudding
stops midair.
"Audition?"
"Me and Alison," I tell her.
"At the Ridgley Community Theater."
"You never said a word," says Mom.

"Remember all the cackling?"
Dad's eyes boggle. "You're auditioning
to play a chicken?"

FEELING IN CHARACTER

Later, Mom asks me what I'm going to wear
for the audition.
I show her Mr. Wilmire's old black T-shirt.
She wrinkles her nose. "I can do better."
She pulls a dress from the back of her closet.
It's satiny black.
Mom sighs. "It'll never fit again.
You may as well get some use out of it."
I try it on.
I look more like a witch.
I start to feel more in character.
I start to believe the audition will go well.
I start to imagine what people will say about me
when they hear I'm in a real play.
I go to my room, stand in front of the mirror.
I practice a pose for when
the *Ridgley Post* photographer comes
to take *my* picture.

BUTTERFLIES AND CROWS

Alison and I walk into the theater.
She says her stomach is all butterflies.
She says that's a good thing.
My stomach is more like
crows in a tornado.
Not good.
I quickly run to
the ladies' room.

THE AUDITION

A guy in jeans and a tie-dyed shirt
writes down our names and ages.
He tells us where to sit—
row 10 with eight other kids,
three of them boys.
There are some grown-ups
in row 11.
Parents, I think.
The woman in row 3
stands up, faces us.
"Hi, everyone," she says.

"I'm Giselle. I'm the director."
She starts bringing kids onstage
one at a time.
Most read from a script.
One boy has his lines memorized.
A girl in purple recites a poem.
Alison and I go last.
Alison tells the director
we are going to do a scene together.
"Sure," says Giselle. "But do the scene twice
so I can focus on one of you at a time."
It's hard to tell, but I think
things went better the second time around.
Especially my cackle.
I wonder which of us
Giselle was watching then.

BRAVISSIMO!

Afterward,
Giselle gathers us all in a side room.
She applauds.
"*Bravissimo!*" she goes. "Good job, actors."
Then she leaves.

The guy in jeans and tie-dye
tells us they will be casting four kids—
two girls and two boys.
"When can we expect a call?" asks a parent.
"Sometime Tuesday," says the guy.
He thanks us. He gives us a thumbs-up.
"Good job, people."
Alison pokes me in the ribs, whispers:
"He's looking right at us!"

WANDERING

With the audition over,
I can focus on my
Emily Dickinson project.
I start reading the first book
about her.
But my mind keeps wandering
back to how it felt being onstage.
To Giselle using her first name
with us kids like we were
real theater people.
To the guy in jeans and tie-dye
looking straight at me and Alison.

The phone rings.
Even though it's not Tuesday,
my heart does a flip.
Mom calls to me:
"It's Mrs. Harden. She wants you to
go over for a minute."

AT MRS. HARDEN'S

Mrs. Harden wants to move her desk
closer to the window.
"Think we can do it?" she asks.
"Sure," I say. "It's not that heavy."
I flex my arm muscle.
After the desk is in place,
we sit down to iced tea and cookies.
(No raisins.)

I tell Mrs. Harden about the audition—
how well I think it went,
how wearing Mom's black dress
got me more into character.

"Now I need to focus on being
Emily Dickinson
for Tuesday's Tween Time," I say.

Mrs. Harden has an idea.
"Think of Emily as a role you're playing.
Dress the part as you're reading about her.
Try to get into the poet's head and heart."

I like that.
"But I don't have a white dress," I say.
Mrs. Harden grins. "I do."

THE WHITE DRESS

I'm a little nervous about taking
the white dress that
Mrs. Harden brings me.
It's the one from her treasure chest—
her mother's high school graduation dress.

Mrs. Harden says her mother would
have loved the idea—

a young friend wearing it as part of
a project on Emily Dickinson.
"Mother loved poetry," she says.

SWISHING

Funny how a dress can change
how you feel.
When I wear Mom's black dress,
I feel more like the witch in *Snow White*.
Now, slipping into Mrs. Harden's white dress,
I feel kind of like Emily Dickinson,
more able to focus on her life.
I stand in front of the mirror.
I turn, swishing.
I swish over to Ottilie's tank.
"Want to learn about Emily Dickinson?"
I say.
Ottilie swishes her tail.
That has to mean yes.
I start reading about Emily.
Aloud.

BEING EMILY

All weekend I work on
my Emily Dickinson report.
I'm down to two poems.
Which shall I read?
"*I'm nobody!*
Who are you?"
or
"*Hope is the thing*
with feathers."
"I'm nobody" is probably
more famous, but it's
kind of a downer.
I don't want to depress
the audience.
I'll go with "Hope."

CAT AND MOUSE

On Monday morning,
I hear Parker yelling outside.
Cape flying—he's chasing after
Shady the cat.

I see the cat scoot under
Mrs. Harden's porch.
"Why are you chasing the Kims' cat?"
I ask.
Parker scowls. "I think that cat
caught a mouse."
"That's what cats do," I tell him.
"But I saved Mousey!"
"You did?"
"Yeah. I scared that cat and
I helped Mousey get away!"
I pat Parker on the head. "Good for you."
"Just doin' my job," he says, flapping off.

ALISON'S COSTUME

Alison comes over after lunch.
She opens her suitcase
and shows me her Sarah Bernhardt costume:
Blue dress with ruffles and puffy sleeves.
Three long strands of plastic pearls.
Her Snow White wig.
(Miss Bernhardt had dark hair.)
And a wide-brimmed navy blue hat

with a peacock feather.
"Wow!" My eyes go wide. "I know where
you got the wig—but what about the rest of
the stuff?"
Alison grins. "Borrowed it from the Ridgley
Community Theater.
They have a great costume closet."
"They actually let you take something from it?"
"I told them it was for a project—community
service."
"Bull," I say.
"Hey, I'm part of the community."

SPIDER-KID

Dad's in the garage
tinkering with a lawn mower.
I'm in the living room with Mom,
reading about Emily Dickinson.
Suddenly Mom screams.
Parker comes running.

Mom points a trembling finger.
"Sp-spider—"
It's sitting on the stack of newspapers—
smack on Parker's picture,
on his nose.
Parker puffs his little chest.
"Don't worry, Mommy. Hero Boy
will save you."

He lifts the top section of the paper
and carries the spider out the front door.
I hope he remembers Dad said, Don't kill
spiders.
They eat other bugs.

Parker does remember.
He dumps the spider over the porch railing
onto the grass.
Then he stands posing by the front door.
He looks up and down the block.
He says: "Today I saved Mousey.
And Mommy. And a spider.
Where's that newspaper lady?"

IT'S OVER

I feel kind of sorry for Parker.
The newspaper lady has
more important things
to write about now.
Nobody wants to read about
spiders and mice.
Parker can flap around
in his cape
and save every mouse
and spider
in Ridgley,
but his fifteen minutes
of fame
are over.

NOW

And now it's
my turn.
Probably a part in the play.

I bet that reporter will be there at
The Foggy Bog Murders
on opening night.

And of course—
my birthday.
Whatever Mom bakes that day
will definitely not
have raisins.

And there's
the Phillies game.

I'm so excited
I keep Ottilie up
half the night
talking.

TUESDAY-MORNING PHONE CALL

The phone rings.
Could it be Giselle?
Would she call this early?
Did I get the part?

Mom pokes her head
in my room.
"It's for you, Suzy Q."
My heart flaps.
I pick up the phone.
It's Alison.
She has a question:
"Are we walking
to the library
as Sarah and Emily
or getting changed there?"

GOING FIRST

Alison and I carry
our outfits to the library.
We get dressed in
the ladies' room
with the other Tween Time girls.

Besides Sarah
and Emily,
there's a Florence Nightingale
and an Annie Oakley.

Ms. Mott greets us as
Harriet Tubman.
She carries an old railroad lantern.
The one boy is Chief Joseph.
Ms. Mott asks who wants to go first.
I raise my hand.
Ever since the audition
I've been feeling more
confident.

I AM EMILY DICKINSON

"I'm the poet Emily Dickinson,"
I tell the group.
"I was born on December tenth,
1830.
When I was a young girl,
I did regular stuff.
I went to school and to parties.
I liked to sing and draw
and play the piano.
I wore pretty dresses. All colors.
When I got older,
I stayed in my room more,

writing poems.
If I did go out,
it was only to my garden
or to visit my friend Susan
across the yard.
I helped in the kitchen.
I enjoyed baking.
Sometimes I lowered
gingerbread and other treats
from my window—in a basket—
to the neighborhood kids.
I had a dog, Carlo.
In my later years
I wore only white.
I died on May fifteenth, 1886.
Most of my poems
weren't published until after
my death.
I'll read one now."

HOPE

"Hope is the thing with feathers
That perches in the soul.

And sings the tune without the words.
And never stops at all.

"That's the first stanza
of the poem called Hope.
I chose this one
because I've been
feeling grumpy lately.
But now I'm not.
Now I've got hope
perching in my soul."

Ms. Mott leads
the applause.

ANNIE OAKLEY

Annie Oakley tells
how she was the star
of Buffalo Bill's
Wild West show.
She pulls out two
cap pistols.
She twirls them

round her fingers.
She points them
at the ceiling.
POP! POP! POP!
I expect
one of the grown-ups
in the library to hiss
SHHHHHH!
But no one does.

FLORENCE NIGHTINGALE

The girl who is dressed as Florence
says she didn't have much time
to prepare because
they had a house full of
out-of-town company
over the weekend.
She tells us that
Florence Nightingale's parents
hated the idea
of her becoming a nurse.
And then the girl
opens up

a toy nurse kit
and gives each one of us
a Band-Aid.

SARAH BERNHARDT

Sarah, aka Alison,
glides to the front of the room
like she's getting an Oscar.
She tells how Sarah Bernhardt bought
her own coffin
and sometimes slept in it
instead of her bed.
She says it helped her
to understand
her tragic roles better.
"Creepy," says Annie Oakley.

HARRIET TUBMAN

Ms. Mott—as Harriet Tubman—
goes next.

She tells how she escaped
from slavery
and helped others escape
using the Underground Railroad.
She sings a song she loved:
"Swing Low, Sweet Chariot."

People from other parts
of the library
come and stand in the doorway
listening.

CHIEF JOSEPH

We all get a little teary-eyed
when Chief Joseph says:
"Hear me, my chiefs; I am tired.
My heart is sick and sad.
From where the sun now stands,
I will fight no more forever."

Ms. Mott passes around
a box of Kleenex.

A LITTLE EARLY FOR HALLOWEEN

Alison and I are too anxious
about Giselle's phone call
to take time to change our clothes.
We wear our 1800s outfits
down the streets of Ridgley.
Some teenagers call out a car window:
"A little early for Halloween!"

RUNNING HOME

After I leave Alison,
I start to run home.
It's not easy running
in a long dress.
I nearly catch my foot
in the ruffled hem.
Whew! I would not
want to ruin
Mrs. Harden's mother's
graduation dress.

So I speed-walk instead.
When I go into the house,
I hear Mom on the phone
saying: "I'll tell her."
"Wait!" I yelp. "I'm here."
But Mom has already
hung up.

WATCHED POT

The phone call
was for me—
but it wasn't Giselle.
It was Alison
asking if I'd gotten
the call yet.
I pull up a chair.
I sit by the phone.
Dad walks past,
pats me on the head,
says: "A watched phone
never rings."

FINALLY!

I stop watching the phone.
It rings before dinner.
It's Giselle.
She is saying nice things
about the audition.
"You did really well, Suzy.
I especially enjoyed your cackle.
I hope you'll try out for us again."
"Again?" I say.
"For another play," says Giselle.
"Gee, everyone was so good. But
we only needed four kids.
Hard choice. Really hard choice.
I'm sorry."
My heart crumples.
I go up to the bathroom.
I turn on the tub water full blast
so no one will hear
my stupid sobs.

TUB TALK

Mom taps on the bathroom door.
"You okay in there?"
"Uh-huh."
Somehow she knows
not to ask about the phone call.
She says: "You're taking a bath?"
"Yeah, I was hot and sweaty."
"Five minutes till dinner, sweetie."
"I'm not hungry."

POOR ALISON

I'm in bed
reading about Emily Dickinson.
Mom brings me dinner on a tray.
I wave it away.
Mom takes my hand in hers.
"I'm sorry you didn't get the part,"
she says.
I shrug. "I feel worse for Alison."
"You do?"
"Yes. She's the one who wants to be

an actress."
Mom gives a sigh. "What makes you think
Alison didn't get the part?"
"We auditioned together," I said.
"Would Giselle really take one of us
and not the other?"
As soon as I say it, I know.
Mom squeezes my hand.
She tells me: "Alison got the part."

SLEEPLESS

I can't sleep.
I get up and walk over to Ottilie.
"I didn't get the part," I tell her.
She swims to the glass
like she wants to hear more.
I go on.
"Giselle liked my cackle," I say.
"But not enough, I guess."
Ottilie's mouth forms an O
like "O, I'm sorry to hear that."
I sniffle. "Alison got the part."
Bigger O.

I blow my nose.
I go back to bed.
I can't sleep.
O.

BLUE WEDNESDAY

I don't feel like
going down to breakfast,
but I do anyway.
Mom hovers over me:
"Want some French toast?"
"Want a banana smoothie?"
"Want to come with me to
Dr. Ellis's today? Borrow some books?"
Dad reads aloud from the sports page—
an article about the Phillies.
Parker whines. "I want to go to the game
tomorrow."
I snap. "It's not your birthday."
"Be nice, Suzy Q," says Mom.
I grab half a bagel and stomp
to my room.

PEP TALK

I give myself a pep talk:
Okay, so you didn't get the part.
Tomorrow is still your birthday.
There will be presents.
And buttercream cupcakes—
no raisins.
Dad and you are still going
into the city. Overnight.
You're still going to see
your favorite team play.
In person!
You may even be able to
get some autographs.
Things could be
a lot worse.

WORSE

Did I say it could be
worse?
Well, it is.
Today started out okay:

It's my birthday.
I've already opened my gifts
and eaten two cupcakes.
I've called Alison to congratulate her
on getting the part
and to thank her for the present
her dad dropped off:
The Collected Poems of
Emily Dickinson.
I'm wearing my Phillies
charm necklace—a gift from Gilbert.
Dad and I are halfway to the city.
His phone rings.
He pulls over.
It's Mom.
She's hysterical.
Parker is missing.

TURN BACK

We turn back.
Dad says we'll probably
find Parker
at one of the neighbors'.

And then maybe we can
get on the road again.
I keep my mouth shut,
but I'm thinking:
the way my life has been
going lately—
fat chance.

WHAT KIND

And now I feel guilty.
What kind of sister am I?
Mad that Parker is missing
instead of worried.
What kind of sister?
The word "rotten"
comes to mind.

SOBS

When we get home,
Mom runs from the porch.
She's crying.

Her shoulders are shaking.
She practically falls into
Dad's arms.
"He's nowhere!"

NO SIGN

Mom tells us:
"I was in the attic gathering up books
for the library sale.
Parker was watching cartoons.
I checked on him twice.
And then—like *that*—
he was gone."
She says she looked in the garage
to see if he had taken his trike.
The trike is still there.
She called Franky's mother.
No Parker.
She checked the closets
and under every bed.
Mrs. Harden checked her closets too.
Mr. Kim drove up one street
and down another.

Gilbert rode his bike to the park.
Alison's mom ran in and out
of all the local shops.
No sign of Parker.

NOT CARING

I think of all those
awful news stories—
kids kidnapped from
their own front yards,
bedrooms even.
I don't care anymore
that it's my birthday.
I don't care that I won't
see the Phillies play.
Or sleep in a hotel.
Or order chocolate chip pancakes
from room service.
I just care that
we find my little brother.

FEATHERS

Dad says: "I'm going to the police station."
Mom says she'll wait at the house
in case Parker comes home.
I go with Dad.
We don't say a word
to each other.
I see some sparrows
at Mrs. Capra's feeder.
I'm reminded of that poem
Emily Dickinson wrote:
"Hope is the thing with feathers."
I am hoping so hard for Parker to be safe
that I wouldn't be surprised to see
feathers on my hands
instead of fingers.

AT THE POLICE STATION

Dad and I go into the police station.
We walk down a noisy hallway
and who do we see walking toward us
but Parker!

He's holding hands with a lady officer.
His shoes are muddy.
There are purple stains on his shirt.
(We find out later they are
grape Popsicle drips.)
And he's wearing his cape.
When he notices us,
he comes running.
He leaps into Dad's arms.
"I got losted!"

TO THE RESCUE

Officer Claire tells us what she knows.
Seems when Parker went to change channels

on the TV,
he saw a news story about a fire at
Deena's Doggie-Groom Shop.
It was in Westville, the next town over.
People were rushing in to bring out the dogs.
Parker figured the shop needed Hero Boy's
help too.
He ran through backyards and down alleys
and up unfamiliar roads,
the cape flying at his back.
But he couldn't find Westville—
or his way back home.
Then he saw some little kids playing
in a sandbox.
They invited him to play too.
When the mother came out to check on
her kids,
she saw Parker, who told her he was lost.
She contacted the police.

REUNION

Dad calls Mom right away.
She's waiting on the porch

when we pull into the driveway.
She runs to the car
and scoops Parker into her arms.
She showers him with kisses.
She twirls him round and round.
She says: "Mommy was so worried!
I couldn't live without my Parky!"
And then she tells him:
"You're grounded.
For life!"

DEFINITELY

I agree.
Parker *should* be grounded for life.
Maybe two lifetimes.
I thought he'd been kidnapped.
I thought I might never see him again.
When all it was
was this dumb hero stuff.
Mom tugs Parker's starry cape off.
"No more Hero Boy," she tells him.
"My sentiments exactly," I say.

ANYPLACE I WANT

It's way too late to go to the city—
the Phillies game has already started.
Dad says: "We'll reschedule, honey.
Somehow.
I promise.
I'll just need some time
to save up again
for those seats we wanted.
Maybe early September."
Big deal.
September is only
a century away.
Dad tweaks my cheek.
"For now, how about a fancy
birthday dinner—
anyplace you want to go,
anything you want on the menu."
"No thanks," I mumble.
And I go to my room.

BAD CHOICE

I'm in the bed.
Thinking.
Feeling.
Remembering when birthdays
were happy.
Remembering the day I read
"Hope is the thing
with feathers."
Bad choice.
I should have gone
with "I'm nobody."

TAP, TAP

Dad taps on my door.
"Phillies are winning," he says.
"Want to watch the game with me,
birthday girl?"
I don't answer.
I pretend to be asleep.

Later,
Mom taps on my door.
She comes in, wakes me
from my fake sleep.
She has a tray of
heart-shaped sandwiches.
And a root-beer float.
And a sign that says
HAPPY B-DAY, SUZY Q
in big red letters.

"Did Dad tell you?
Maybe September now."
"Yeah," I grump. "If the little hero
doesn't run off to save the world again."

Mom sets the tray on my desk.
She drapes her arm around me.
"I'm so sorry, Suzy Q.
What a bummer of a birthday.
But don't worry—when Dad
gets new tickets,
I'll bar the doors.

I'll handcuff the little hero
to my own wrist.
He won't get away,
I promise!"

"Whatever," I say.
Mom kisses the top of my head.
She leaves the tray.

I don't eat a bite.

ALONE

Alison calls.
I refuse to go to the phone.

Parker sings "Happy Birthday"
outside my door.
I hold my ears.

Ottilie burbles.
I don't even want to
talk to Ottilie.

I just want to be
left alone
in my room.
Forever.
Like Emily Dickinson.

MY FIRST POEM EVER

Emily didn't title her poems—
though sometimes she referred to them
by their first lines.
Her poems have numbers.

I print the number *1*
at the top of the page
and then:

I'm nobody. Who are you?
Whoever you are—
well, toodle-oo.
Don't bother me.
Don't write or phone.
Adios! Goodbye!
Leave me alone!

THIS TIME

Last night, I dreamed again
that I was Emily.
This time—
carefree and floating
in a long dress
through the backyard
by moonlight.

AFTER THE DREAM

I ride my bike
to Goodwill.
I buy three white dresses

(probably from someone's
prom or wedding).

At home,
I change into one
with pearl buttons.
I look perfectly Emily—
except for the Phillies cap.

I toss it like a Frisbee
into my closet.
I don't even feel bad.

CALL ME EMILY

At lunch, I make my announcement.
"Call me Emily from now on."
Parker gives me a look. "Huh?"
Dad butters a roll, says:
"Suzy's pretending to be
Emily Dickinson."
I let the word "pretending" slide.
"Who's Emily Dickensomething?"
asks Parker.

"A famous poet," says Dad. "From long ago."
"Oh," says Parker, no longer interested.
Mom curtsies. "And what would Emily
like to drink with lunch?"
"Hot tea," I say in my new Emily voice.
"Cup and saucer, please.
No mug."

ROSES

After lunch, I go out to the yard.
I snip two roses.
Mrs. Harden sees me.
"Don't you look pretty," she says.
"Thank you," I say.
I give Mrs. Harden one of the roses.
And then I hurry inside.
(Emily was shy. Even with the neighbors.)
I fill a vase with water.
I put the rose in it and set it on my desk.
What would Emily do now?

SKIMMING PAGES

One of my birthday gifts—
from Mrs. Harden—
was a thick biography
of Emily Dickinson.
I open it.
I skim for things
Emily did with her time
after she became a recluse.
I make a list:
Write letters.
Write poems.
Play the piano.
Bake.
Read.
Make breakfast.
Wash dishes.
Dust.
Tend the garden.
Care for sick mother.
Play with dog, Carlo.
Listen to crickets.

LETTERS

I go with
Write letters.
One to Alison.
One to Gilbert.
I'll explain things
in case they
start wondering
why they don't
see me around
anymore.

DEAR ALISON

I know you are going to be
very busy with the play.
I'll be busy too:
writing poems,
reading,
baking,
sewing . . .
stuff like that.
Also, I'm going by

the name of Emily now.
And I'm no longer
taking phone calls.
Only letters.
Real ones.
Your busy friend,
Emily
(formerly Sooze to you)

DEAR GILBERT

This is to let you know
that the ice cream offer
is off.
I'm really sorry.
I'll be spending a lot
of time alone now.
You won't be seeing me,
unless maybe by accident.
Also, I've taken on
the name of Emily.
I do hope you'll write.
Real letters.
On paper.

You can leave them
in the basket on the porch
if you don't have stamps.
Your friend,
Emily
(formerly Suzy)

NO PIANO

So far,
I've written one poem
and two letters.
I decide to follow Emily's list
in order.
Next, *Play the piano*.
We don't have a piano.
I go to Parker's room.
"Lend me your xylophone."
He digs it out from his toy box.
I take it back to my room.
I play "Twinkle, Twinkle, Little Star."
Over and over.
Dad pokes his head in the doorway.
"Know any other songs, Suzy?

I mean, Emily.
I think we're just about
twinkled out."
I roll my eyes, give a loud sigh-groan.
"'Twinkle, Twinkle, Little Star' it is, then,"
says Dad, backing away.

NO VISITING

Next it's Mom who stops by my room.
"I have to drop something off at Dr. Ellis's.
Want to come with me?"
"I don't go visiting," I tell her.
"But I'd appreciate your mailing these
while you're out."
I give her the letters I wrote
to Alison and Gilbert.

WHO'S OTTILIE?

A few minutes later,
Parker pops by.
It sure isn't easy

to be a recluse
in this house.
"What do you want?"
I ask.
"I want to visit Ottilie."
"Who's Ottilie?"
Parker folds his arms
across his chest.
"Your goldfish, dummy."
"My goldfish is named Carlo,"
I tell him.
Parker stomps out. "You're
getting me all mixed up,
Suzy."
I scream after him:
"I'm Emily!"
He screams back:
"Sooooooooozie!"

SATURDAY IN THE KITCHEN

Mom tells us all to stay out of
the kitchen.
"I'm going to clean and
organize the cupboards."
"But I was hoping to bake," I tell her.
"You?" she says. "Or Emily?"
"Mom," I groan. "I *am* Emily."
Mom closes her eyes, blows a strand of hair
from her face.
Then she takes her apron off the hook
and drapes it over my head.
"Make way for Emily," she says,
and leaves the kitchen
to me.

GINGERBREAD MISSION

I send Parker
over to Mrs. Harden's
for her gingerbread recipe.
"And don't you dare
go anywhere else," I say.

"I'll be watching you
from the window."

WRONG APRON

Parker comes back
with the recipe
and a letter
from Mrs. Harden.
I tuck the letter
in my pocket.
I'll read it
after I bake.
But I can't bake
in this apron.
It was a Christmas gift
from Grandma Fludd.
It's got a huge cactus
with Christmas lights
all over it.
Emily would never
wear such a
monstrosity.

Her apron would be white.
I dump the cactus.

BACK IN MY ROOM

When the gingerbread is done,
I wrap squares of it
and take them to my room.
"Can I have a piece?" Parker asks.
"Not now," I tell him.
I close the door.
I read Mrs. Harden's letter.

DEAR EMILY

Thank you for the lovely rose.
It's in a vase on the kitchen table,
reminding me of you.
Remember, my dear,
Emily Dickinson did leave her house
on occasion
and walk across the way
to visit her sister-in-law

and dear friend, Susan.
Perhaps I can be
that kind of friend to you.
Come visit.
Anytime.
Fondly,
Mrs. Harden

SATURDAY EVENING

I do remember.
Emily's brother, Austin,
married a woman named Susan
(which used to be my name).
Emily could easily slip over
on moonless nights
and not be seen
by anyone.
Maybe on some dark,
moonless night
I will slip over
to Mrs. Harden's.
But not now—
the sun is still out.

SOME KEEP THE SABBATH

On Sunday morning, Mom asks
if I'm ready for church.
I reply, quoting the first two lines
of an Emily Dickinson poem:
"Some keep the Sabbath going to Church—
I keep it staying at Home."
Mom looks at her watch.
"You've got thirteen minutes."

SUNDAY CLOTHES

I come downstairs
in my long white dress.
Dad gawks at me,
then at Mom.
"She's wearing *that*?
To church?"
Mom shrugs.
"I've seen worse."

RECLUSE-ING AT CHURCH

It's as hard being a recluse
at church
as it is at home.
Everyone in church
is friendly.
A couple people
ask about the dress.
"From the thrift shop,"
I tell them.
They are polite.
They don't ask
any more questions.
The pastor's wife says that
I look "quite pretty."
The custodian asks
if there's a wedding
he doesn't know about
on today's schedule.
He chuckles at
his own humor.
Mom says I can skip
Sunday school
and stay for the sermon,

which I do.
Afterward, I sit in the car
while the rest of the family
heads for the coffee hour.
I see Gilbert and his mom
walking across
the parking lot.
I crouch down so
they won't notice me.
Finally we go home.
I race to my room,
shut the door,
and flop on the bed.
Who would have thought
being a recluse
could be so
exhausting!

REQUEST

Franky comes over to play
with Parker.
Parker knocks on my door.
I open it a crack.

"What?"
"Can me and Franky have
some gingerbread, Suzy?"
I shut the door.
Parker knocks again.
"I mean some gingerbread, *Emily*?"
"Go stand under my window," I tell him.
"And wait there."

FOOD DROP

I look out
to where Parker
and Franky
are standing—
like I told them—
right below
my window.
I put two
wrapped squares
of gingerbread
in the lidded basket
I found in the attic
and lower it

with a rope.
Parker opens the lid.
Franky grabs
the first piece.
He unwraps it.
He takes a bite.
He spits it out.
"This stinks!"
he calls up to me.

FORGOT

I slam the window shut.
What does a little kid
know about gingerbread,
anyway?
I unwrap a piece
to taste for myself.
It stinks.
I think I forgot
the sugar.

NEXT

Next on Emily's list:
Read.
Easy.
I take down *Jane Eyre*,
a popular novel in the 1800s.
I decide to read aloud
to Ottil—oops—I mean, Carlo.
I haven't been paying
enough attention to her
lately.

A SURPRISE

Later in the day,
I realize
I never pulled my basket
back up.
So I do.
It feels a little heavier
than when I lowered it.
I open the lid.

Out pops
a chipmunk!

TERRIFYING

I'm not usually afraid
of chipmunks.
I think they're cute.
But when one pops
out at you—
in your bedroom—
it can be terrifying.
I let out a scream.
Dad comes running.

CHIPPY

I stand on a chair
and point toward
my desk,
where the thing
darted.

"Chipmunk!" I screech.
Dad gets down on
his hands and knees,
peers behind my desk.
"Chipmunk—" he says.
"Here, Chippy . . . Chippy . . ."
Chippy doesn't show.
Dad tells me to go get a bucket.
"Don't drown the little thing,"
I plead.

WAR ROOM

"Drown what?" says Mom,
coming into my room.
Parker and Franky follow.
Dad yells: "Close the door!"
I say: "There's a chipmunk
behind my desk."
"I want to see!" says Parker.
"Somebody get me a bucket,"
Dad says.
"And a towel too."
"Chipmunks bite," says Franky.

"I'll get the bucket," I say.
"I'll get the towel," says Mom.
"Take the boys with you," says Dad.
"Don't get rabies, Mr. Quinn,"
says Franky.
"Out!" says Dad.

CAPTURE

I come back to my room
with the bucket,
Mom with the towel.
Dad tells Mom and me
to move the desk
from the wall.
We do.
Dad corners the chipmunk,
which scoots right into
the bucket.
Dad flips the bucket up
and slaps the towel on top.
He goes to stand up
and hits his head on the desk.
He says a bad word.

"I heard that, Daddy," says Parker,
who is in the hall with Franky.
"Be quiet," Mom tells him.
Dad takes the bucket
out to the backyard
and sets the chipmunk free.

OUT OF PATIENCE

Dad's head is bleeding.
Mom pulls him
into the bathroom.
She cleans the wound
with a washcloth.
I hear Dad say,
"I'm running out of
patience with
this Emily thing."
Mom tells him
to hang on a little longer.
I figure I'd better
smooth things over.
I check my Emily list.

Next is *Make breakfast*.
I can't wait till morning.
"How about I make supper
tonight," I say to Mom.

MAKING AMENDS

I make ham steaks
with pineapple,
one of Dad's favorites.
Also green beans.
And for dessert
chocolate-mint ice cream.
Dad has a lump on his head,
but he's cheery during the meal.
After supper, he gets up. "I'll
do the dishes."
I give him a hug. "I'll do it.
Wash dishes is next on my list."
Dad looks at Mom. "List?"
"Don't ask," she says, pulling him
into the living room.

APPROVAL

On Monday morning,
I *dust*,
then *water plants*.
Mom tweaks my cheek.
"I'm beginning to like
this Emily."
Parker tugs Mom's skirt.
"Hey," he says, "what about me?"

EMILY'S WAY

The phone rings.
Mom hands it to me.
"It's for you."
I back away.
"Who is it?"
"Alison."
"Tell her to write."

A HALF HOUR LATER

The phone rings again.
Dad tells me, "It's Alison,
and it's an emergency."
This time I take the call.
"What's the big emergency?"
Alison giggles. "I miss you."
"Put it in writing," I say.
"That's goofy, Sooze. You are
not Emily Dickinson."
"I never said I was Emily *Dickinson*."
"You're not Emily *anybody*."
"People change their names all the time."
"Whatever," says Alison. "So—want to
go to the dollar store?
They're having a half-price sale."
"I don't go places," I tell her.
"You went to church."
"Mom made me."
"You're just being goofy."
"Then don't call anymore."
"Maybe I won't."
"Fine."
"Fine."

OF COURSE

Of course she'll call.
Alison wouldn't know
what to do
without me.
I'm her best friend
in all the world.
I bet she stops by
to try to trick me
into seeing her.
Any day
now.

THREE DAYS LATER

No call.
No letter.
No tricky visit.
"Alison must be
sick in bed,"
I tell my goldfish, Carlo.
"With a really,

really bad
summer cold."

LOOKING

I go into the kitchen.
Mom looks up from
her iced tea.
"Aren't you hot in that
long dress?" she asks.
"Not at all," I say,
peeking into the freezer.
"Looking for a Popsicle?"
"No," I tell her.
"I'm looking for chicken
to make broth
to send to Alison.
She must have a terrible cold."
"I don't think so," Mom says.
"I saw her this morning
at the dollar store.
She looked fine to me."

BIKES

I decide to go for a bike ride.
But nowhere does it say
Emily Dickinson ever rode a bike.
I don't even know if they
were invented back then.
Dad's in the driveway,
tinkering with a lawn mower.
"Hey, Dad," I say. "When
were bikes invented?"

OH

Dad loves answering questions
about history.
He sets down his wrench.
"Da Vinci sketched a bike
in 1490," he tells me.
I brighten. "Ah, so there *were*
bikes in Emily Dickinson's time."
"Well," Dad says, "the da Vinci sketch
stayed in his notebook. But there were
bikes in Emily's day."

"Yippee!"
Dad goes on. "They were called
boneshakers.
They had huge front wheels.
A person mounted the bike like a horse."
"Wow!"
"One thing, though."
"What?"
"Only men rode boneshakers."
"Oh."

NICE DRESS

Mr. Kim comes
up our driveway.
He must be having
lawn-mower problems again.
Before I can scoot away,
he says,
"Hi, Suzy. Nice dress."
I keep walking.
"Are you in
some kind of show?"
he calls.

I go into the house.
I shut the back door.
Hard.

DAD'S MAD AT ME

When Mr. Kim leaves,
Dad comes up to my room.
"You were rude to Mr. Kim,
Suzy."
"I'm not that name," I say.
"Mr. Kim doesn't know a thing about
this phase of yours," Dad says.
"It's not a phase. I'm being Emily."
"Well, your Emily may have been eccentric,
but she wasn't rude."
I want to say: How would you know?
You weren't there.
But I don't.
Dad leaves.
He closes the door,
not so gently.
I throw my pillow
against the wall.

SEWING

I mope in my room
for an hour.
No calls.
No notes.
No visitors.
Not even Parker.

I give a sigh.
I check Emily's list:
Sew.
Yikes!
I haven't sewn
since I was six
when Grandma Quinn
from Oregon
helped me make
a pot holder
for Mom.

Then I remember—
my favorite
Phillies shirt
has a rip in the seam.

I was going to ask Mom
to fix it for me
before I turned myself
into Emily,
who only wears
white dresses.

Still—it's something to sew.
I dig it out of the dresser:
my Phillies shirt.
I almost get weepy—
a relic from
my other life.
I rub it against my cheek.

NO MORE TICKLE MONSTER

It's almost dark.
Mom comes upstairs.
She tells me that she and Dad
are going over to Mrs. Harden's
to fix a leak in her kitchen.
I'm in charge of Parker.

I make sure he gets into his pj's
and brushes his teeth.
I ask if he'd like me to
read him a story.
"No," he says. "I want Tickle Monster."
"Then good night," I say.
Parker wails. "I want Tickle Monster!"
"Good night," I say again.
"It's not *good*," he sniffles.
"It's a *poopy* night and it's all
your fault!"

ANOTHER DAY AS EMILY

I wake up thinking about
Tween Time
and wonder if Alison
will go without me.
She only joined
in the first place
because I coaxed her.
Whatever.

Who cares.

Dad is acting
mostly normal.
Not mad like yesterday.
I ask him if he'll deliver
a letter to Ms. Mott
on his way to work.
He says yes.
But he doesn't tweak my cheek
or try to tell me some
post-office trivia
from back in the day.

Who cares.

I check the porch basket.
No letters for me.

I hear Gilbert whistling
as he passes my house.

Parker is going
with Franky and
his family
to the pretzel factory.

Who cares.

THANKS FOR ASKING

I feed Carlo.
I make my bed.
I sit by the window
and look out.
Then back to Emily's list:
Care for sick mother.
Mom is sitting
at the kitchen table
with her coffee
and her nose in a book.
"How are you feeling today?"
I ask.
She looks up. "I'm fine. But
thanks for asking."
"You look a little pale," I tell her.
She smiles. "No makeup yet."
"How about a nice cup of tea
to perk you up?" I say.
Mom lifts her coffee mug. "I've got this."

"Are your shoulders stiff?" I ask.
"Would you like a shoulder massage?"
"Can I take a rain check on that?" Mom asks.
"As soon as I finish this page
I have to call Dr. Ellis."
"Sure," I say.
"Great," says Mom.
I pat her on the back.
"Feel better soon."
And I head to my room.

NOT SURPRISING

Emily Dickinson seemed to enjoy
playing with her dog, Carlo.
Not surprising—since you can
actually do stuff with a dog:
Teach it tricks.
Take it for a walk.
Play fetch
or tug-of-war.
Groom it.
Pet it.

Enter it in shows.
Even volunteer it
for work in schools
or nursing homes.
Try doing any of that
with a goldfish.

THE LAST THING ON EMILY'S LIST

Listen to the crickets.
Well, I can't do that now.
It's only 9:30 a.m.
I go back to
Read.
I pick up *Emma*
by Jane Austen.
I remember how much
I liked the miniseries.
No TV for me anymore,
though.
Ah well—don't grown-ups
always say
the book is better?

LUNCHTIME

I read.
All.
Morning.
Long.
I decide
not to wait
until noon
for lunch.
At 11:49
I hear something.
Visitors?
I peek downstairs.
It's just Mom
dusting the living room.
"Emily Dickinson
hated to dust," I tell her.
"Hmmmm," says Mom.
"I think I'll get some lunch,"
I say.
Silence—except for
the swish of the dust cloth.

"Anything good
in the fridge?" I ask.
"Pasta salad."
"You think Emily Dickinson
ate pasta salad?"
Mom stops dusting.
She gives me a look.
I know that look.
"Pasta salad it is," I say.

GRUMPS

I eat by myself.
Then it's back to my room.
I tell Carlo about Dad and how
he hardly spoke to me at breakfast.
And now Mom—all grumpy.
And Alison—some friend she turned out to be.
"What is wrong with people?" I say.
Carlo swims into her underwater castle.
No comment.

I GUESS I'LL WRITE A POEM

Emily wrote a lot about
the stuff around her.
The garden.
A bird outside her window.
A clock.
A fly.
She also wrote a lot about
death.
I guess I'll stick to
the stuff around me.
Here goes . . .

POEM ABOUT THE STUFF AROUND ME

Here's to my goldfish,
my desk, and my chair.
Here's to the sneakers
I no longer wear.
Here's to a hair clip,
a comb, and a mug.
Here's to the fly

that is dead
on the rug.

DEATH AFTER ALL

I guess it's all part of being
a poet—
this death stuff.
Even without meaning to
I got it into my poem.
I have a title for another
death poem.
How about
"Bored to Death"?

Except
I'm too bored
to write it.

READY

Time is a worm.
It crawls.

How did Emily
stand it?
I'm ready to
wimp out,
crack up,
give in,
and go back to being
plain old Suzy.
Then Mom comes up
to my room.

SUPPER INVITATION

Mom tells me that
the Capras
have invited
all the neighbors over
for lasagna
and homemade
ice cream.
"And live music,"
she says.
Mr. Capra's nephew
is bringing his guitar.

I shrug.
"Sounds like fun,"
says Mom.
"I can't go," I tell her.
Mom throws her hands up
into the air.
"Of course you can go."
"I'm Emily," I remind her.
"I stay home."
Mom takes a deep breath.
I wait for her to coax
just a little.
But she doesn't.
She simply says,
"Suit yourself."
And goes out the door.

MAYBE THIS TIME

Mrs. Capra sends Dad home
with a plate for me:
lasagna, salad, and bread.
Also a small container of
strawberry ice cream.

I wait for Dad to coax me
to come over.
One teeny-tiny coax
and I might topple.

But Parker is with him,
yanking at his shirt.
"Let's go, Daddy.
We're missing all the fun!"

MUSIC AND LAUGHTER

I take a couple bites
of lasagna.
And a spoonful of ice cream.
But I'm not hungry.

Music and laughter
spill across the air
into my window.

I slip into my nightie,
into my bed.
I pull the sheet
over my head.
Still the happy sounds.

But do you think
anyone,
anyone at all,
is asking,
"Where's Suzy?—
I mean, where's Emily?"
Ha!
Fat chance of that.

SAD

My heart feels like an egg
that has cracked—
sad is seeping out of me.

A tear is rolling down my cheek.
But who cares?

I MUST HAVE DOZED OFF

When I wake up, it's 10:07 p.m.
Mom and Dad are whispering in the hallway.
Mom: "We need to do something."
Dad: "Yep. It's time."
Mom: "Can't ground her."
Dad, chuckling: "She's grounding herself."
Mom: "It's not funny."
Dad: "The surprise should do it."
Mom: "Suppose she says no?"
Dad: "We'll cross that bridge
when we come to it."

WHAT SURPRISE?

No way can I fall back to sleep.
What surprise are
they talking about?

Hmmm . . . maybe they are
going to ship me off
to Grandma Quinn's in Oregon
for the rest of the summer.
Well, I won't go.
I love Grandma Quinn.
But Emily Dickinson
doesn't travel.

NO DOUBTS

The next morning,
I'm back to being Emily
without those
sad little doubts.

Just let my parents
try to
surprise me with
a trip out west!

AT THE DOOR

I'm eating breakfast
when there's a knock at the door.
Mom peeks out the window.
"It's Gilbert," she tells me.
"I can't see visitors," I whisper,
choking on my toast.
Mom blows out a long
I-can't-stand-this-much-longer
breath.
She opens the back door.
"Emily can't see you, Gilbert."
I whisper: "Tell him to leave a note."
Mom glares at me. "*You* tell him—"
and walks away.

THE BIG SURPRISE

I stay behind the open door.
"What do you want, Gilbert?"
Gilbert pokes his head around.
"I have a surprise. Good news."
"What?" I say.

"I'm going to a Phillies game.
Against the Mets.
August eleventh."
My heart sinks.
I try not to show it.
"Wonderful," I say. "I'm happy for you."
"My dad won tickets from
a radio talk show.
He was the thirteenth caller
with the right answer."
"Really," I say.
I am ready for this conversation
to end.
"Don't you want to ask me
how many tickets he won?"
I'm seeing something sneaky
in his eyes.
"And how many tickets
did he win, Gilbert?"
Gilbert doesn't speak.
He just holds up fingers.
Four of them.
My heart is picking itself up
off the floor.
"Four?" I say.

Gilbert ticks them off
one finger at a time.
"Me.
My dad.
You.
Your dad.
They're great seats too."
I'm halfway out the door.
I want to scream.
I want to hug Gilbert.
I want to turn cartwheels.
But I don't.
I'm Emily.
I say to Gilbert:
"I'll have to
think about it."

DEBATE

You can't go.

Why not?

Emily Dickinson would never go.

How do you know?

Baseball wasn't a big deal then.
Emily probably never even heard of baseball.
And she never went to a game.

But why?

Too many people. Crowds of people.

Maybe she had a good friend we don't
  know about.
Maybe that friend dragged her to a
  game once—
just to get her out of the house.

You believe that?

No.

A VOICE

I go from hugs and cartwheels
to a rotten mood.

Dad brings me a note from Ms. Mott.
I toss it aside.
I don't tell him about the baseball game.
There is also a note
in the porch basket—from Alison!
I toss that aside too.
I tell Carlo:
"I'm having a really,
really hard time
being a recluse."
I flop onto my bed.
I close my eyes.
I punch the mattress.
I hear a voice.
Where is it coming from?
The hall?
My head?
The fish tank?
It says: Then don't be one.

DARK

I think it will
never come again—

the dark.
But it does,
and I creep over to Mrs. Harden's
to talk things over.

BE SUE

Mrs. Harden beams
when she sees me.
She whisks me inside
and gives me a hug.
"I've been thinking about you,"
she says.
She points to her craft table.
It's cluttered with paint
and brushes and rags.
She holds up a poster.
Glued at the top
is a picture of me
in my Phillies cap.
I read the words
below the photo—
BE SUE WHILE I AM EMILY.

I stare at Mrs. Harden.
"Huh?" I say.

IN BLACK AND WHITE

Mrs. Harden opens a book
of Emily Dickinson's poems.
She begins to page through them.
"It's a little piece of advice
to her best friend whose name is—"
She looks at me.
"Susan," I say.
"Exactly. Ah, there it is—"
She points to the first line
of a poem.
"Why don't you read it
out loud," she says.
I keep staring at the words.
Finally I speak:
"Be Sue while I am Emily . . ."
Mrs. Harden is smiling at me.
"Sue," I say.
"Susan," she says.
"Suzy," I say.

"It's like"—Mrs. Harden reaches out
and touches my face—
"she wrote those words for you
those many years ago.
She left a message for you."
Mrs. Harden's smile
is getting blurry.
"For me."

I BREEZE IN

Back home,
Mom and Dad
and Mr. and Mrs. Kim
are in the dining room
playing Scrabble.
I breeze into the room.
"Who's winning?" I ask.
Mom and Dad exchange glances.
Mrs. Kim points to her husband.
"He had the *z* and the *x*."
I give Mr. Kim a big smile.
And a thumbs-up.
Mom says, "Uh—want to join us?"

"No thanks," I chirp.
"I'm going to hang up this poster
Mrs. Harden made for me.
Maybe another time."
Mom's mouth is hanging open—
she gawks.
Dad just shakes his head.

UPSTAIRS

I hang the poster
above my desk.
I get into my nightie.
I slip my red Phillies shirt
over the nightie
and find my Phillies cap.
I brush off a dust bunny.
I get the letters
I tossed aside earlier.
One from Ms. Mott.
One from Alison.
I read them aloud
to Ottilie.

MS. MOTT'S LETTER

Dear Miss Emily,
We missed you at Tween Time today.
Please consider coming next week.
I will set a chair behind the bookcase
for you.
You may have all the privacy
you like.
Just come.
Yours respectfully,
Ms. Mott

ALISON'S LETTER

Hey, Sooze,
Remember me—
your best friend?
Guess what?
Giselle is looking for a helper,
someone to be "on book"—
that's when an actor forgets his lines
and the person on book reads the lines back.

Also to do other stuff around the theater.
I thought of you right away.
Doesn't this sound like more fun
than being a twelve-year-old hermit?
Call me!
Alison

SOUNDS LIKE FUN

It's too late to call Alison now.
But I do like the idea.
I never really wanted to be an actress.
But this—this does sound like fun.
"Good night, Ottilie," I say,
climbing into bed.
I trace my mouth with my fingers.
I'm grinning.
I'll tell Dad in the morning
about the game.

1:15 A.M.

I can't sleep.
I grope through my room
in the dark
down the hallway.
I open
my parents' bedroom door.
I listen to them breathing.
I call out:
"We're going to a game!
A Phillies game!
August eleventh!
Against the Mets!
We're going to a Phillies game!"
I close the door.
I go back to my bed.
I'm asleep in a minute.

WHEN I WAKE UP

The first thing I think about
is Emily's list
and what activity
I'm going to choose—
and then I remember!
I'm not Emily anymore.
I'm *me*.
Suzy Quinn.
I grab the list
and tear it
into tiny pieces.
I toss it in the air—
confetti!
And go down to breakfast.

AT BREAKFAST

Mom is scrambling eggs.
She eyeballs my Phillies shirt.
No comment.
"Want toast with your eggs?"
"I'll make it," I say.

"Okay."
"Where's Dad?"
"Left early for a class."
"How about Parker?"
"Went to Franky's for the day."
Mom spoons scrambled eggs
onto my plate.
"Funny thing—
your father and I
had the same dream
last night.
You were standing
in our bedroom
shouting something about
going to a Phillies game."
I sprinkle salt
on my scrambled eggs.
"It wasn't a dream," I say.
"Gilbert's father won tickets.
They're taking me and Dad."
My mother dumps
the rest of the eggs
onto her plate.
"And Miss Emily—would she
go to a Phillies game?"

I start gobbling down my eggs.
"Emily?" I say. "Emily who?"
Mom freezes.
She gapes at me—
with big eyes,
kind of like Ottilie does.
A couple seconds like that
and then she gets it.
"You're Suzy again?"
"The one and only," I say.
"Yahoo!" she yips.
And yanks me out of the chair
and we go dancing around
the kitchen table.

ON BOOK

When I call Alison,
I half expect her to tease me
about the Emily Dickinson business.
But she doesn't.
She just gives a happy squeal
that I'm willing to be on book
or whatever

for Giselle.
"Rehearsal's at six p.m.,"
Alison tells me.
"And don't be late.
Giselle hates late."

BIKE

I'll call Gilbert later,
tell him yes to the game.
I'll reply to Ms. Mott
later.
Right now,
I just want to ride my bike.
I go out to the garage.
There it is—leaning against
Dad's workbench, all red and shiny.
Dad must have been
keeping it dusted.
I lay my head on the handlebars.
"Hello, sweet thing," I whisper.
I wheel it outside into the sunlight.
I hop on.
I ride into the golden light,

the warm breeze,
away from the houses.
I pat the bike.
"Oh, wouldn't Emily Dickinson
have loved you," I say.

THE DAY FLIES

I'd forgotten
what a busy life
I used to have.
Mrs. Harden invites me to lunch.
She teaches me how to make
strawberry salad and poppy seed dressing.
I go on Mom's computer and catch up on
all the latest Phillies news.
Alison calls. She wants me to come over.
"I'll do your hair," she says. "You can
have supper here.
We can go to the theater
together."

AT THE THEATER

Giselle explains more about
being on book.
When an actor forgets a line,
the actor calls "Line,"
and then I read the line
as it is written.
I'm not supposed to give a line
unless it's called for.
Giselle asks me to sharpen
some pencils for her.
I also help move scenery,
find props.
And fix Giselle's coffee—
two sugars, no cream.
Rehearsal is over at nine.
Giselle asks me to flip off
some of the lights.
"Good work, Suzy," she says.
Alison sidles up to us. "Don't forget
who got her for you, Giselle."

SUDDENLY

Alison's father drops me off at home.
Mom and Dad are watching TV.
"How'd it go?" Mom asks.
"It was cool," I say.
"I love working at the theater."
"Gilbert called," says Dad.
"Thanks," I say.
Then: "Where's Parker?"
"In bed, I hope," says Mom.
I laugh. "You never know with
the little hero."
I grab the feather duster.
I tiptoe up the stairs.
I think I'm going to Parker's room—
but I don't.
Suddenly there's something
I have to do.

THE BLURT

I detour into my parents' bedroom.
I pick up the phone. I dial.

I don't even sit on the bed.
As soon as Gilbert says "Hello?"
the words burst out.
"I'm coming to the game.
Of course I am.
What was I thinking?
I don't even know what happened,"
I tell him. "One day everything was normal,
and the next day Parker was a superhero—
newspaper stories,
a medal,
a parade,
and what was I?
I was the little hero's sister.
Boring old Suzy Quinn.
Nobody wanted to meet *me*.
Nobody took *my* picture.
And then I went to the audition—
and didn't get the part.
But I learned about acting and
I read about Emily Dickinson
and I figured, hey, why should I be stuck with
boring old Suzy Quinn when I could be
a famous and fascinating recluse?
And for a while it seemed like it was working."

On and on I go. When I finally stop,
I'm gasping as if I just finished a race.
Gilbert laughs.
He absolutely *howls* on the other end of
the line.
"Suzy"—he says—"*that* was a major blurt."
I try to join in the laughing, but it's hard
because it takes breath to laugh.
When I finally calm down, I say:
"I guess what I mean is—I missed myself."
There's silence on the other end.
I wonder if Gilbert has put down the phone.
Then he says: "I missed Suzy too.
I'm glad she's going to the game."
When we hang up, it feels like two
holding hands
coming apart.

MONSTER

I pick up the feather duster.
I tap on Parker's door.
"Who's there?" he asks.
"Guess," I say.

"Emily?"
"No."
"Suzy?"
"No."
"I give up."
I open the door.
I creep
step
by step
over to Parker's bed.
I wave the feather duster at him.
"It's the
Tickle Monster!"

A WORD ABOUT EMILY DICKINSON

Emily Dickinson was born in 1830.

Celebrated today as one of America's greatest poets, Emily, in her own time, was better known as a gardener. A niece once remarked that Emily's garden had enough blossoms to gorge "all the bees of summer." When Emily sent a verse to a friend, it was often attached to a bunch of flowers.

When she wasn't tending her garden, Emily could often be found in the kitchen of the family home in Amherst, Massachusetts. Her specialty was baking. She once won a prize in a bread competition with a rye and Indian round bread.

Emily was not a very social person. Her brother's wife, Susan Gilbert, was perhaps her best friend. She also loved her dog, Carlo.

As Emily got older, she became more and more housebound. Visitors might find themselves speaking to her from the other side of the closed front door. From her bedroom window she would lower baskets of gingerbread to the neighborhood children. When someone did manage to get a glimpse of her, she was always wearing white.

No one in Amherst knew how much time Emily spent with her poetry.

She had little interest in publication. Fewer than a dozen poems appeared in print during her lifetime. After Emily died in 1886, her sister, Lavinia, discovered nearly eighteen hundred poems locked in a chest. At Emily's request, Lavinia destroyed all of Emily's correspondence after her death, but preserved her poetry so that it can still be read today.

EILEEN SPINELLI is the beloved author of nearly fifty children's books. Among them are the middle-grade novels *Summerhouse Time* and *The Dancing Pancake* and picture books such as *Cold Snap* and *Princess Pig*. Eileen and her husband live in western Pennsylvania. When Eileen was ten, she used to drape herself in her grandmother's old white organdy curtains and recite Emily Dickinson's poem "I'm Nobody! Who Are You?" in front of the mirror (making sure no one was watching!).

JOANNE LEW-VRIETHOFF's passion for art has given her the opportunity to illustrate picture books and middle-grade novels for the last fifteen years. She lives in Amsterdam with her husband and two wildly imaginative kids. Learn more about Joanne and her work at joannelewvriethoff.com.